WildStreak

By
Theodore Potter

PotterHouse Publishing LLC
Tok, Alaska 99780

For information, email the author at:
potterlwen@hotmail.com

Copyright © 2012 Theodore Potter
All rights reserved.
ISBN: 978-0-9799567-2-0
0-9799567-2-2

DEDICATION

For Fern, My loving and talented wife.

FOREWORD

While trying to shut out the sixty eight below zero temperatures in the winter of 2007 and not get a case of the preverbal cabin fever living in our cabin in Tok Alaska, I pinned three western novels called Claim Jumpers, Guns, Gold and True love and this book, Wildstreak. Of the three my pick would be Wildstreak.

Randy Earl Mulehouse, who at first appears a hapless cowboy is quick on the draw and seems to meet some of the most gorgeous woman whom he marries. The first takes off with his heart with another man, while the other three succumb to different illness's that are fatal.

Randy's way of handling each sudden end to his marriages is found in a ninety cent bottle of whisky. This leads to a Wildstreak that lasts for months and extenuating circumstances that lead into other relationships with another woman.

Theodore Potter

CHAPTER 1

The rider reached for the canteen hanging on the pommel of his saddle, brought it up to his ear and shook it. There was very little water in the thing. The cowboy got down off the horse and took his hat off and poured half of the water in it, about a cup. He said to his horse, Sniffer, "Old girl, we're almost down to our last drop."

His mount nickered at him and sniffed the hat. He took some on his hand and wet the horse's nose then let her drink the remainder. The pony sucked the last bit of moisture from the silk lining of the hat.

Randy Earl Mulehouse took a small sip from the canteen and hung it back in its place. He gazed at the desolate scene before him. He could see the Superstition Mountains off in the distance to his right and when he turned west with his gaze he could almost imagine seeing the outline of the Gila River where it flowed as it meandered through the desert from the foot hills of the Weaver Mountains.

He hoped water would be there at the great bend of the river, aptly named Gila Bend. The last time he had been there water covered most of the valley. It was only a small Mexican settlement, but that was four years ago. Maybe the town hadn't changed, but his circumstance had changed since then for sure.

Now he was a loner once again and didn't have a clue as to where he was bound. He had tried his luck at settling down with a woman, but with each passing day, she had become more and more unresponsive to his attempts to even talk to her.

Then one day he rode home from his job as a cow puncher and found his wife gone from their place and a note pinned to the door that read; "I'm leaving, don't follow me!" In town he was told she had caught the stage to Denver with her bags, in the company of some carpet bagger.

Well, he thought that's that. He rode back home, gathered up his livestock and drove them into town. He sold them at pennies on the dollar. He found the marshal and told him what happened; if anyone wanted to buy the place, just make an offer and put the money in the bank. He gave the marshal the deed. He knew him to be an honest man.

The marshal tried to talk him out of going, but he didn't blame Randy one bit for leaving. That woman had been right down mean to Randy and Randy had tried his best. If he tried to stick it out here now, he would make himself crazy. He had a nice little place out there and someone would come along and buy it.

The small ranch was in northeastern New Mexico. Randy had moved there from Kansas and landed a job punching cows for one of the largest outfits around back then; the Shipley Ranch. The Shipley's had been wonderful to work for and had made it possible for him to own a small piece of land that bordered the ranch.

The year had been 1862 and Baran Shipley was one of the most successful ranchers in the west. When Randy's wife of four years took off, Baran had tried to get Randy to move over to the ranch full time as a Forman, but his woman's leaving had put something wild in him and he apologized and went on his way.

Now he was in a pickle, if there wasn't any water in that river, he and his horse might die. He led his mount at a walk towards what he knew was the closest approach to the river. The trail led through the Maricopa Mountains and then sloped down to Gila Bend. He still had some miles to travel; it was sure hot for winter time and the heat sucked juice from a man's body quickly.

He was jolted out of his reverie by a sound that had grown out of his consciousness, from a barely discernible thing, to a full scale team moving fast coming up on his rear. He mounted his horse and stood in the middle of the trail waiting for the stage to arrive.

The team of eight horses came into view and they were moving fast. The driver saw him and began trying to stop the team. Randy moved over and let the stage pass him. It stopped a hundred feet farther on. The driver stood in his box looking back and declared, "You will get yourself run down young man, don't you know that."

The man said it with a grin however and added, "Come on and I'll get you some water for that sorry excuse of a nag you're astride of."

The wizened old driver got down and went to the rear of the coach and took down a liter bag of water and filled Randy's canteen and a bucket about half full for the horse. He carried on a running commentary all the time. He filled two more buckets and handed one to Randy and said, "One draft each, pointing down the right side of the team."

Randy did as he was told and met the driver at the head of the team. The team of horses seemed to have this operation down pat and not one of them tried to over draft on him.

He looked at this driver and liked what he saw. The man was somewhere between forty and sixty, but looked in excellent shape. They walked back to the rear and as they passed the carriage a beautiful face appeared at one of the windows and almost scared him to death. The woman inquired of the driver if they were in Gila Bend yet. The man said, "No honey, just had to stop and rescue a cowboy that's all."

The female said. "A real cowboy."

"Yes, and he will ride up here with me Salena and not back there where you can put silly notions in his head."

The girl said. "Oh Uncle Bill, you are so mean, do you know that?"

The two men climbed up to the lofty seat of the coach laughing, then Bill talking a blue streak, got the team under way. He said, "That's my sister's kid back there, Salena Townsend, she has been back east getting educated. Her mother has a spread just west of Gila Bend in the Gila River Valley."

Randy let Bill talk until he ran down, then Bill finally ask Randy what in thunder he was doing way out here without a good supply of water. Randy replied that the last time he had been through here, it rained so much that the river was out of its bank and looked more like an ocean than a river. Bill said, "That would be back in fifty-eight wouldn't it? There is almost always either more or less water than we need out here and never seems to be just right."

The trip down the other side of Maricopa Mountain was easy on the team and the two men talked comfortable about many things. Finally Bill asked him what he wanted to do out here in this desert. Randy was silent for a spell and then decided this man would become his friend and told him about his wife leaving the way she did and his subsequent departure from his little ranch in eastern New Mexico. It was Bill's turn to be silent. He had had much the same thing happen to him and had been a confirmed bachelor since. Finally he said. "You seem a good sort to me, why don't you stick around the Bend for a spell, there is work aplenty and I think I can point you towards a punching job; if you are interested."

Randy thought maybe that wasn't such a bad idea and told Bill so. Bill said. "You can bunk at my place until you sort things out if you want."

Randy didn't want to hurt this man's feelings so he accepted with grace. Bill said. "Well now, that's settled isn't it?"

CHAPTER 2

Bill's place was amazing to Randy. It was an old stable that Bill converted to living quarters. The floors were scrubbed clean, but he could still smell the stable smell of horse manure. Bill told him he wouldn't even notice it in time and much to Randy's surprise he was right. The place was nice and well kept. Bill explained his sister came to town pretty often and looked after the place for him. He spent many hours on the high seat of the Wells Fargo Stage. His next run was Yuma and return. He told Randy he would stop and fill his sister in about him and when she came in town, if he wanted, he might ask her for a riding job.

Randy thanked him and went to take care of his horse. He stripped the saddle and blanket off and found a curry comb and worked the mount down. The horse enjoyed his administrations a great deal and nickered at him in thanks. Randy rubbed her ears and went in search of Bill. He found him in his kitchen making coffee on a wood cook stove. It was hotter than a goat in a pepper patch in the kitchen. Randy went back outside.

He noticed the town of Gila Bend hadn't grown one solitary bit in four years; it just had more people who had done as Bill had and converted some vacant places to live in. There was still more Mexicans than white folks, but they all seemed to get along with each other. The hot bed of activity was the Mexican style Canteen down the street. Randy wasn't a drinker, but a cool beer would sure taste good in this heat.

He told Bill where he was going and walked down the dusty street. The town had a feel of Old Mexico. The Canteen was one quarter mile down on the opposite side of the street.

The interior was cool and dark. As he entered, a hush fell on the few patrons of the bar. Randy walked with ringing spurs up to the bar and sat on a stool. A young Mexican boy came over and said, "Hello senior, what would the senior wish to drink?"

Randy said, "A cool beer if that's possible." The boy ducked back of the bar through some curtains and came back with a jug of beer. He put a beer glass on the bar and filled it up. There was a small head on the beer. Randy picked the glass up and found it to be cool. He turned the glass up and emptied it. He sighed and told the boy to fill it up once more. The boy stood there and didn't move. Then Randy remembered he hadn't paid the boy. He reached in his vest pocket and put a five dollar gold piece on the bar. The boy smiled and filled his glass and when it was empty he filled it again. Randy told him, "That's my limit son and I'll nurse this one."

The boy put the beer away and brought four paper dollars and eighty-five cents in change. Randy put a dime on the bar for the boy. This caused the boy to grin from ear to ear and say, "Thank you senior, thank you."

The noise resumed in the Canteen and music began playing over in one corner. Randy walked over to a table with his beer and sat down facing the piano player and settled back and listened. The player wasn't very good, but he knew a lot of songs and seemed to get better as time progressed.

It snuck up on Randy that things weren't right somewhere behind him. He turned and found what looked like a mixed breed Mexican glaring at him. Randy smiled at the man, but his eyes shifted away and looked at some distant thing. Randy turned towards the man with his body, but put his eyes back on the old man playing his songs. Randy heard the chair scrape back and heavy footsteps coming his way. The breed squared off in front of him and leered at him through drunken eyes. Randy asked gently, "Can I do anything to help, my friend?"

The breed spit out, "I don't like you Gringo."

Randy shrugged his shoulders and replied with, "I'm very sorry mister, but I don't think I like you very much either."

Randy had his gun under the table ready to fire. He said, "Maybe you should go home and sleep it off my friend."

The breed saw he was losing the battle of wits and clawed for his gun. Randy's forty-four went off just as the breed's gun cleared leather. Randy's bullet took the breed in the chest at the brisket and he was dead on the way to the floor.

Randy came out of his chair and rolled on the floor as a bullet whistled over his head. The shooter was the dead man's friend, and when his friend died, he decided to shoot Randy in the back and would have, if Randy hadn't dove for the floor and turned in time to see him. The surprised look on the gunman's face was because he knew he was going to die. Randy drilled him right dead center and the luckless man fell in a heap.

There were two more men in the bar, but they held their hands up away from their side arms. Randy said to the boy peeping over the bar, "Sorry son I couldn't help it, those two men were looking for trouble."

The boy rose up and solemnly said, "And they found it senior."

He scampered through the curtains and returned with the beer jug. He grinned and said. "This one is on the house senior."

Randy asked the boy, if there was a Marshal in this town. The boy shook his head no, then volunteered that there was an undertaker of sorts. One of the men said, "I'll go get him."

Within five minutes a tall bean pole of a man entered the Canteen and approached Randy. He asked matter of factly "You do the killing Mister?"

Randy replied with. "Not by choice sir."

The undertaker replied with. "That's good to hear sir. Too many times that's not the case here in the west. I'll bury these two for the worldly processions they happen to have on them. Then if there is any claim on them for bounty, you will have that. I'll send their particulars into Yuma and find out in a day or so. Sorry you have had such a poor welcome to our little town."

He and the two men took the two bodies out of the Canteen and the piano man resumed his playing. The curtain parted and a girl of maybe twenty-two or three came out and moved to Randy's table. She said, "I am sorry those men treat you badly sir."

Randy smiled at her and said, "I'll bet you they are sorrier than I am seniority." He added that she should set down and she did.

Randy asked her name and she answered Mareio Counjours and that she owned this Canteen, then he told her his name. She said. "Those two bad men have been causing trouble for me and my brother and I'm glad they are gone, thank you very much."

He took her hand and something of an electric shock went through the both of them. Mareio was suddenly flushing in the face. Randy thought he had never seen a Mexican blush before, but here it was. They hung on holding hands until her brother saw what was happening, then both let go. She whispered. "Come see me late tonight. I have my own entrance on the rear. Make it after closing time." She brushed his arm heavily with her ample breast as she got up to leave.

Randy sat there for a spell and thought about what had just happened. He was for sure attracted to this girl and her to him, but he didn't know if he was ready for what she had in mind yet. He had loved his wife right up to the moment she had, behind his back, slipped out from under him and went to someone he supposed she had met somewhere. He decided, he would come back after closing and at least talk to this beauty.

There wasn't any reason to be rude to her and she looked to be an arm full.

Bill greeted him, "Looks like you been busy young man."

Randy sat down and told Bill what had taken place at the Canteen and Bill said. "Well you probably rid Gila Bend of two pieces of rubbish and you'll only be respected for that around here. How about some chow? I fixed some beef and beans on the stove over there, help yourself."

Randy realized he was hungry and fixed himself a plate then came and sat across from Bill. The beans and beef were hot with peppers, but delicious and he cleaned his plate. Bill told him, "I have to make the Yuma run come morning, want to ride along?"

Randy thought for a moment and said. "By golly I will if it's ok."

Bill said. "Five o'clock we leave."

Randy said. "There's something I have to do tonight, but I'll be there come morning Bill."

He left and went to the rear of the Canteen and knocked lightly on Marieo's door. The door was jerked open and there stood Mareio in a short night dress. He lost all the reserve he had made up in his mind and went inside. Two hours later he came out the door and felt only a second of remorse that he had been weak for a moment.

He reasoned in his mind, that his wife was lost to him forever and he vowed to himself he would get a divorce in Mexico, across the border when he reached Yuma.

At four-thirty in the morning Bill rousted him out of the bunk he had loaned him and poured him a cup of coffee. The heat of the wood stove felt good this morning and the mesquite wood it burned put a pleasant odor in the air of the old stable. They were out of the stable by 4:45 am., and the team was already harnessed and hitched up to the stage over at the stage depot. As Randy passed the stage passenger doors, a head stuck out and a sweet voice said. "Well, good morning you handsome cowboy."

Randy stopped and looked up at what could only be described as one of the most beautiful faces he had ever seen. He said. "Good morning miss, how are you today?"

She answered with. "I'm tired after my uncomfortable night at the stage stop. I had no idea a bed could be so lumpy or saggy."

Bill had come up to them then and all three laughed. Bill said. "Salena I tried to get you to come over to my place and you refused."

Salena said. "I don't like the smell of your place Uncle and as far as I'm concerned it will always be a stable."

Bill said. "Aw, if you spent a little time there, you'd get used to it and not even let it bother you."

Salena mumbled to herself, maybe I'll try the next time I come to town.

The stage left Gila Bend right on schedule at five am. There were three other passengers besides Salena. Two were older women and the other was some kind of fancy dressed gambler. The gambler had been in Gila Bend since last week, putting up at the stage house. He had tried getting a game up while there, but found no one with money, that wanted to play poker with him. He liked the girl, but was far too old for her and didn't try to engage her in any way. The two older women were as stolid as statues and hadn't said one word since they had all wound up at the Wells Fargo stage house. The Yuma stage only ran once a week, so that stage house had been like a prison to the gambler. He was glad to be on the move at last. He simply pulled his hat down over his eyes and went to sleep.

Noon found them at their first stop at the Sentinel stage house. The horses would be changed out and everyone fed a meal. Bill, Randy and Salena sat at a table together. It was pretty obvious that Salena was for sure gone bonkers over Randy and couldn't keep her eyes off him. Randy liked what he saw in the girl, she was near twenty or so and as pretty a one as he had ever seen, but he was sitting here with her uncle and was on the way to find a job with her mother. He had to be cool or he might ruffle some feathers. As soon as it was prudent he got the heck out of there.

He found the Gambler out near the stage. He spoke to the man and was spoken to in return. The gambler said. "You may not realize this young man, but you have turned that young lady's head around in there."

Randy looked at the man and replied with. "Yes I know and it's not to my liking either sir. That's her Uncle Bill driving our stage and her mother owns a ranch somewhere along here and I'm supposed to work for her, I hope. You can see I have to be careful here."

The gambler smiled and said. "You have more fortitude than I do sir. I'm afraid if I were in your shoes, I might have to scoop her up and race her off somewhere."

Randy decided he liked this fellow and the two talked until it was time to resume their trip.

Randy saw the two horses and woman as they topped over a long rise. He correctly assumed this to be Salena's mother with a mount for her. Bill pulled up and got down, he said, "Hello sister, I have someone here you might want to have work for you. He comes highly recommended."

Bill introduced the two by saying. "Joanlea this is Randy, he has traveled with me since the Maricopa Mountains and he rid Gila Bend of a couple of pieces of trash last night. I think he should accompany you to the ranch and if you don't hit it off, it would surprise me a bunch." Joanlea shook Randy's hand.

She was handsome woman of forty-eight or nine and had some gray in her long hair. Her look was cool and said volumes to Randy, like, "show me and we'll be Ok". Randy got his horse from the rear, mounted and the three rode north while the stage thundered west towards Yuma.

CHAPTER 3

The two women and Randy rode for almost an hour before he asked Joanlea how far it was to her ranch. Joanlea and the girl stopped and laughed. Randy began getting red in the face. He felt he was the brunt of some kind of a joke or something. Joanlea smiled and said, "We were on my land where you got off the stage, Randy."

Randy saw the humor in it then, and laughed along with mother and daughter. Randy felt a little more at ease after that and began to enjoy himself.

The ranch house and out buildings came in view at last and took Randy's breath away. The shallow valley where the ranch lay was absolutely beautiful. The Gila River ran through the valley and had many pools of water that gleamed in the sunlight. The house was built on the highest ground in the valley and was a long low structure that formed a large L.

The closer they got to the house the more beautiful it seemed. The walls were stucco and almost a red color. The roof was green tile that must have been brought in from Europe or somewhere. Randy couldn't keep his eyes off the house as they rode towards it.

There were a few cows sprinkling the fertile fields of green grass, along with more than a few horses. Randy said. "Lots of horse's mam."

Joanlea replied with. "We are essentially a horse ranch, but keep a few head of beef around. The Apache Indians here about are called the Mescalear and come here along the Gila River as a god given right. I have an understanding with them for the most part, they leave my horses alone and I give them a live beef or two now and then."

Her statement made Randy really feel good, because he was a good part Indian himself, although not the fierce kind at all. He had been raised in Oklahoma in the Indian Nations and was one-third Cherokee with a bit of Irish and a heaping of Scotch thrown in to solidify the mess. This woman had prospered in the middle of a tribe that more or less would never give in to the demands of a race of people that seemed to want it all and didn't much care who they tromped on to get it.

They rode to the barn and Randy started realizing how big everything was here. The house had grown larger the closer they got. He was amazed that someone would build something this beautiful way the heck out here.

The barn was huge as well and some hands met them and took their horses. Joanlea said. "Randy, I would like you to be our guest for dinner tonight so we can talk if you want."

Randy wanted to very badly and told her so. Salena clapped her hands and said. "Oh goody, we haven't had company in a long time have we Mom."

Joanlea said with a smile, "You have been away for three months daughter; maybe while you were gone I moved a tall dark handsome man into my boudoir."

Salena got red in the face and told her mother she should be ashamed talking like that in front of a guest. Randy was tickled and began laughing. He was sure glad this diva had a sense of humor.

They went in the house and if Randy had been impressed with the outside he was astounded that a house could look this good inside, out here in the desert.

The floors were hardwood and the walls were some sort of paper that had pictures all over it. He had never seen anything like it. Joanlea was a most gracious hostess and catered to his every need. They had installed him in a beautiful room on the east side of the house where it was cool and some Mexican had drawn him a bath that he needed pretty bad.

He had clean clothes in his saddle bags and when he came out from his guest room, Salena let go a wolf whistle that startled him half to death. He had never heard a woman whistle like that before. Her mother must not have either, because she came running, wanting to know what in heck that infernal noise had been. Joanlea looked at her daughter and declared. "You have picked up some abnormal habits out east haven't you daughter?"

Randy's face was beet red and he felt sorry for Salena who was down cast and wishing she had kept her whistle to herself. He said. "Aw shucks mam, the girl was just having some fun that's all."

He saw Salena looking out from under her bowed head with mischief in her eyes and thought, oh hell, she's got it bad.

Joanlea asked Randy what he would like to drink with dinner. The choices were wine, whisky, bourbon, milk, imported beer from Mexico or water.

She was having a good time playing hostess to him and he didn't mind one bit. He had been neglected far too long and he was by golly going to enjoy this night. He said, "I've never tasted most of those and may never do so, but I like beer and someone told me the Mexicans make some pretty good stuff."

Joanlea pulled a strap hanging above her head and a nicely dressed middle aged Mexican glided into the room on silent feet. He bowed to Joanlea and said in flawless English "Your pleasure Miss's and Mr."

Joanlea asked, "Do we have cold Mexican beer Don Jesus?" {Pronounced Hey sues}

Who replied with. "A complete barrel that has been in the cooling cellar for months Miss."

Joanlea said. "We will have a jug of that and some white wine I think, please."

Jesus disappeared as quietly as he came and returned with drinks on a tray. The beer was colder than Randy thought possible way out here and it tasted good.

The evening had progressed well. After drinks, dinner was served in a beautiful dining room that would rival any in the world and the food was delicious and well prepared. There was a large rump of roast beef and all the trimmings. Randy was full long before he wanted to be, but finally sighed and gave up. He thanked his two hostesses for their hospitality and they all retired to the living room. They were all too full of food to drink anymore, so they just talked.

The two women wanted to know all about him and Salena especially wanted to know what a six foot four hunk of man was doing way the heck out west here. Randy told them what transpired to bring him out where the coyotes howl at night.

He was most definitely unsettled by his own admission, but felt he needed to settle down somewhere and make a life for himself. He still owned a hundred and sixty acre ranch back in New Mexico, but didn't think he could stay there after his wife had done him that a way. He was silent for a spell and when he looked up at the two women they both had wet eyes and that startled him. He had always thought his problems with his wife would be of no concern to others, but he had moved this mother and daughter to tears with the simple sad truth of the matter. He decided he had to cheer them up. So he began telling clean jokes he had heard down through the years. Soon he had them both in stitches and they all went to their respective rooms in a great mood.

Morning came with a sweetness he thought he would never experience again. Somewhere a rooster crowed and a cow bellowed. There were birds singing outside his window and the air smelled sweet and cool. The heat of the desert had retreated down below Mexico City somewhere leaving the Mohave Desert cool, like it was supposed to be in the winter months.

There was a gentle knock at his door and a Mexican girl stuck her head in and said. " Breakfast in twenty minutes sir."

He thanked her and jumped out of bed. He was startled so bad he almost pissed himself, when Salena said. "Oh my goodness you look as good without clothes as you do with them."

Randy was glad he hadn't slept in the buff last night, but in his shorts. He said. "Look girl, you just get the hell out of here and let me get dressed."

Salena was sitting in one of the two chairs over by the window and Randy hadn't seen her when he woke up. She looked pouty for a moment and then brightened and said. "I am not sorry I sat and watched you sleep for the last two hours and if that doesn't mean anything to you, then maybe I better look for someone who it might mean something to."

To Randy's astonishment, she then stomped out of the room slamming the door behind her. He sat and thought hell, how many women cared enough for someone that they'd set for hours just watching a man sleep. He felt ashamed he had reacted the way he had and decided to do something about it as soon as he could.

He entered the dining room and found Joanlea alone sitting at the table. He said. "Good morning Mam how are you this fine morning?"

She replied with. "I'm fine thank you, but something has gotten into my daughter since she arrived back from that school."

Randy decided he couldn't let some school back east take blame for what he knew was his fault. He said. "I don't want to do this right now, but I feel you should know what is really wrong with Salena. Your daughter is in love with me I think and I've done nothing to encourage her I promise."

Joanlea said. "If that's true, sir: you better do something about it or get on down the road with yourself."

She was openly staring at him and waiting for his reply. He said. "Excuse me, I must find Salena."

He charged out of the house to the giggles of the mother of his new girlfriend.

Randy found Salena out at the barn cleaning up after horses. He walked in and saw her immediately and went straight to her. The girl stopped what she was doing and faced him as he approached her. She was red in the face and had obviously been working hard. He stopped a few feet from her and spoke. He said, "I have been through so much pain since my wife of three years left me that sometimes I don't consider other's feelings, and this time is no exception. I can see you are one of the most beautiful women this old cowboy has ever had the good fortune to become acquainted with and should; as the gambler on the coach said to me, scoop you up and race you off. The only thing I'm worried about is that I may not be entirely ready for another relationship this early on and you may get hurt. I do want to keep you as a friend and hope someday to fall head over heels in love with you."

He was silent then and watched as Salena's face reflected many different emotions before settling down with one of simple resignation. She walked over to a stack of feed and sat down with her face in her hands. After some time she said. "Don't you even like me a little bit?"

Randy's heart near lurched from his chest. He went to her and took her in his arms. She came willingly and they kissed long and deep. They broke apart and went up the ladder to the loft. There would be no turning back now and he knew it.

That night, Joanlea was beside herself not knowing what took place with the two and finally couldn't stand it one second longer and asked them if everything was Ok. Both smiled at one another and said yes everything was fine. This only added to the mystic for Joanlea and caused her to drink just a little too much white wine that evening. Towards bed time she point blank asked Randy if he had made love to her daughter.

Randy was nonplussed at her directness and took awhile to answer her. Finally he said. "Your daughter and I have an understanding between us that we are not going to push ourselves into a relationship unless we're both certain we're ready for it Joanlea, and I hope that's ok with you."

Joanlea thought to herself; this man had refused her daughter's love and held her at arm's length because he didn't want to hurt her. To Joanlea that was a most honorable thing for a man to do and she respected him for that. She could see her daughter had moon eyes for Randy and didn't blame her one bit. If she were younger she would jump right in the fray.

She had married her childhood sweetheart and came west with him. They had applied for and received a grant of 1,000.000 acres of land in the Gila River valley and built this ranch. Farley, her husband had gotten on a bad horse when Salena was six and when the horse threw him he died instantly from a broken neck. She had never desired another man since and may never in this life; she and Farley had had too much together over the years. She understood Randy's problem. When one loved as he and she had; just because one of the loved ones was removed from the equation, the other didn't stop loving that person. Someone might come along to fill the void, but they would always be in second place. This is a fact of life.

Joanlea thought long and hard about what had to be done about Randy, before she came to a solution. She needed a Forman on the ranch and as far as she could see, Randy would be a good one.

After breakfast the following morning she called Randy outside and discussed the possibility of her making him her head Forman. Randy thought maybe he had lucked out and told her so. Joanlea told him he could have the guest house as his residence. The small house was close to the bunk house. She told him to get settled in and come see her when he was ready to work.

CHAPTER 4

The heat was so intense that the desert shimmied in the sun light and almost would blind a man, if he didn't shade his eyes. Randy had his hat pulled down as far as he could and still it was bright. He and a crew of six had driven a hundred and fifty horses to market to Yuma and were now returning to the Lazy Eight Ranch.

The trail out to Yuma had been dry and they were lucky to not lose any horses. The weather had turned hotter than normal for May and now was about to scorch the riders. The horses suffered most in the heat, but a man wouldn't last long on foot out here.

They were a mile or so from Aztec Springs, when Randy told his men, they had better walk on to the springs now, because the horses were spent. Without a word seven riders swung down to the ground and led the tired horses on foot.

One hour later Randy's mount nickered and wanted to rush forward. Randy said. "Mount up men we can't let these horses have their heads, they'll destroy the spring."

The spring was a small pool in a stand of salt bush and if one of the animals got in there first it would be undrinkable for hours and this bunch didn't have hours left until they would all die of thirst. He ordered them to dismount once again and tie their mounts to a salt bush. Each man knew the drill and took their hat and brought it full of water to their thirsty horses. The water was cool and sweet. The cowboys drink their fill each time they came back to the spring. It was late evening so Randy decided to camp for the night. They went past the springs a half mile and made camp. A fire of mesquite was quickly built and beans put on to cook. Dried beef jerky was soaked in water and boiled to add to the meager meal. The men spread their blankets and went to sleep. None of them even paid any attention to the Coyotes fussing over the scraps thrown out from the meal.

When the sun came up they were on their way. They doubled back to the spring to water up and damn near got scalped for their carelessness. A band of Apache had camped at the spring last night and the only thing that saved them was Randy noticing a small thin curl of smoke rising above the salt bush. He put his finger to his lips and motioned his men back where they had just come from. They would have a dry ride to the ranch on this day.

Once out of hearing, the seven riders rode like thunder while the weather was cool. The ranch came in view just before noon. The women rushed out to meet them and Randy swung Salena up behind and rode to the corral with her. She hugged his back and said, "I missed you Randy."

Randy answered with "I missed you too girl."

Life settled down at the ranch. No more horses would be taken to market this summer, although the US Army would buy all they produced. The weather would be far too hot for driving them to market. The ranch become a daily grind with not much to keep Randy occupied. He became edgy and when he felt he might snap, he went to Joanlea and told her he needed some time away from the ranch. She said "Why don't you draw your pay and go up north somewhere for the summer then come back in the fall and go back to work."

Randy thought that was a grand idea and didn't waste a bit of time getting his gear ready to hit the road. He was packing his saddle bags with clothes when he sensed someone at the door of his house. He glanced up and saw a weeping Salena standing there. He rushed to her and took her in his arms. He said, "I'm sorry honey, but it's better this way and I'll be back come fall. You can be a companion for your mother while I'm gone."

Salena bobbed her head yes, but said. "I'll wait for you forever sweetheart." Then she dodged out the door.

He was left torn between going and not going. Finally Joanlea came in and sat down. She said, "I know what you two are going through Randy and believe me, if you stay you will destroy her love for you. Go and get this wild blood out of you if you can. If you can do that you might make my daughter a good husband someday."

CHAPTER 5

He thought the black hills of Dakota would be cool this time of the year, but not so, the heat and dry air sucked the water right out of a man.

Randy was approaching the trading post at Gillette, Wyoming Territory, the beginning of the black hills over in South Dakota.

The ride up from Denver had been an interesting one for Randy Mulehouse. He had ridden to Tucson with his friend Bill on the Wells Fargo Stage and then rode northeast through the Superstitious Mountains and up through the Apache Nation. He circumnavigated a five mile wide Canyon that was a mile or more deep and went for miles as he rode along its rim going east.

At the bottom of the Canyon was a river that looked fierce even a mile away. He rode north keeping the river in sight. When he came to a point where he could get down to it he wasn't disappointed at the rivers fierceness. He would never swim his horse across that. The water was cold and sweet. He camped for a week along its bank.

The sun was hot during the day but the nights could be bitter cold. He found a natural cave that was only twenty feet deep with a hole in the roof. He lay in pinion fire wood aplenty and rested up. He shot some rabbits and one small deer that wandered too close to camp. He wouldn't starve to death out here. The month was May and up here in the high country summer was still a month away.

He spent the better part of May making his way through Colorado via the old Brigum Young trail. The trail ascended to dizzy heights at times where the air was so thin that breathing was difficult. Sniffer, his trusted horse, would suddenly stop and pleadingly look at him as if to say enough boss. Near the top it snowed and almost froze Randy to death. He wore his bed roll in order to stay warm. As they descended to lower altitude it warmed and spring sprung on him. What a difference two thousand feet of altitude could make in comfort. He dang sure would buy a heavy coat and warm long johns when they reached Denver.

He remembered his Denver shopping trip vividly. He had gone in the western mercantile company to shop and ran smack dab in to his estranged wife. He came near running back out, but with heart fluttering he approached her. She was busy with another customer and he waited patiently for her to notice him. When she finished with the other, she said automatically, "May I help you sir."

She looked him in the eye and Randy thought she was going to faint dead away.

He smiled and said sardonically "Well, this squelches all the rumors that you died, don't it?"

She put both her hands up to cover her face and ran from the room. The manager was right there and wanted to know just what in hell he thought he was doing frightening his wife that way. Randy laughed out loud and replied with, "Well, she might be your wife now, but I have papers that say she is my wife and furthermore, she left me and never got a divorce either."

Randy thought the store clerk was going to croak right there. He sputtered that "You are a damn liar sir and I'll defend my wife's honor."

Randy said, "You will die for your troubles too sir, so don't challenge me, I don't want her back and would rather shoot her than you anyhow."

He walked out and went to another store, bought what he needed and rode north. He was glad he had run in to his wife and her new husband. He was on the way to healing up now.

The new castle trading post was operated by two nice married folk named Lasiter and Jody Holt. They took to Randy and become fast friends. Randy sat down to a table for the first time since leaving the ranch. There were Indians hanging around the post and Randy become friendly with them. He found they were Sioux and a prouder bunch never existed. He sat for hours and talked to Lasiter about everything. Lasiter told him the Army would push the Sioux tribe beyond their tolerance someday and there would be hell to pay when they did.

CHAPTER 6

The town of Deadwood looked like just what it was, a Wild West gambling, drinking; shoot em up place that more or less stayed open all night. Randy rode there because he had been told the weather was always cool at that altitude. There were some gambling halls along Main Street where a man could get in a poker game if he desired. Some men cheated or simply made someone mad and died for their transgression. Most games were peaceful though. He drank beer in the first place he came to and found himself in a game within twenty minutes of his arrival.

He liked poker and wasn't bad at it if he had to say so himself. The game was dealer's choice and they played seven card stud. They played pot limit. Meaning a player could bet no more than what was in the pot. Randy drew a pair of Jacks in the hole and a duce as an up card. He went along with the first bet of five dollars which was the anti as well. His fourth card was another Jack giving him three of a kind and that was a good hand in seven card stud. The bet came around to him again and he raised it five bucks to ten dollars. No one dropped out and this was exactly what he wanted. He still had three cards to draw and his chances were excellent that he would draw a pair and give him a full house or a boat as it was called in the game. When the bet came around to him this time he upped it by twenty bucks and caused one player to fold. All others went against their better judgment and called. The next card was another Jack.

He now held the fifth highest hand in the game. Four queens, kings, aces or a straight flush would beat the hell out of him. He saw no evidence that anyone held as good a hand as he did, so he raised twenty more bucks. Everyone folded but one man. This man had been losing all night and needed this pot to stay in the game. When the last card was dealt down, Randy checked to the other man without looking at it. The man was sweating bullets and decided to go all in. If he lost this hand he wouldn't be able to buy a beer. His money was counted and Randy pushed the correct amount of cash into the pot. The fellow turned his three Kings over like he knew he had won and reached to drag the pot in. Randy grabbed his wrist with his left hand and gently said, "Hold up friend, I don't think three Kings beat four Jacks."

The man locked eyes with Randy and they turned mean. Randy let go of his wrist and turned his four Jacks over. The man's eyes moved down to the cards and back up to Randy's. Randy saw it in his eyes that he was going to draw his gun and in a move so fast nobody saw it, drew his forty-four and killed the man. His opponent had his gun only half drawn. The man slid down to the floor and Randy raked his winnings in and walked out of the place. It was so quiet his spurs rang like bells. Randy got on Sniffer and hell bent, left the town of Deadwood forever. He felt bad that a man had lost his life over a couple a hundred dollars. Randy wished the man hadn't let it go that far.

It was mid July and hotter than he ever thought it would be. He remembered someone telling him about how cool it was over on the west coast. Randy had never seen the ocean and thought he just might like to, so he pointed Sniffer's nose west.

The settlement of Spearfish, South Dakota lay in his path and he would stock with food there, if there was any that is. Near the east end of Spearfish, he pointed Sniffer's nose up a canyon that seemed to go on forever. He grew weary after two or three miles and found an off shoot ravine with good grass for his horse and went to sleep in a fireless camp.

Something woke him from a dream about Salena. The two of them were about to climb a mountain of some kind. He listened intently until he picked up soft breathing of a good sized animal. Sniffer nickered and moved to the end of her rope to be as near to Randy as possible. Randy came out of his bedroll as silently as he could. He moved near his horse and quieted her with a hand on her nose.

His eyes were accustomed to the dark now and he searched for the animal until he found it then pulled off a round just above its head. In the muzzle flash, he saw the mountain lion stretched out in a long leap away from him and Sniffer. Randy was shaking from the chill and the excitement. He gathered wood and made a fire quickly. He knew he had almost become a part of that Mountain Lion's diet. He vowed not to camp without a fire ever again. This would come back to haunt him at a later date.

He was told by some Indians, that he could buy food and whisky over at Fort Bell Fourche {pronounced fuch} a day's ride north west. So he put Sniffer in an easy lope that ate up the miles and when the sun was still high he came into Fort Bell Fourche.

He realized there was a whole lot of nothing out here and somehow that suited him fine. He had killed three men since his wife left him and derived no pleasure from it, but he realized he was done talking and that meant if someone drew down on him he had no recourse, but to out draw him.

CHAPTER 7

Randy needed to spend a few days here, so he checked into the only hotel in town. When he asked the clerk what the name of the hotel was the man just smiled and said, "Ain't got one sir."

Randy laughed at that and asked if the town supported a blacksmith. The answer was affirmative. He went down to the barber shop and bought a bath, haircut and a shave. When he came out on the street again, he felt renewed all over.

All he needed now was a good feed. The great western road house and restaurant was the only place in town that served food, so he aimed himself for it. There were no individual tables, only long tables with benches. The tables were loaded with food and it seemed every puncher from miles around must be eating here at the moment. He almost turned away, but his stomach rumbled and he barged right in and found a place at a table.

The food was surprisingly good. He ate his fill and paid his dollar at the door as he left. He thought that was high, but he wasn't about to complain, because he would want to eat there another time. Back on the street, he took his horse over to the blacksmith to be re-shod. He then went into the livery and found the hostler and bought a feed bag full of grain for Sniffer. Old Sniffer grunted her thanks while she ate the grain.

The town of Bell Fourche fell behind him as he rode through some badlands into Wyoming Territory He had been told the best trail was right through the Rocky Mountains. If he tried going around them he would have to go north to the Canadian border and cross that way and that was a month's longer ride.

He and Sniffer made better time than most horse and riders because they really liked each other and Sniffer took the trail as fast as she was comfortable with. Her mile eating lope wasn't tiring to the superbly conditioned horse.

Sniffer was six years old and had been his since birth. He had bought a mare from the Shipley's and took her home to his ranch. At the time he had no idea the mare was with foal, but she began getting bigger and bigger until Sniffer was dropped. The little foal came to Randy sniffed and sniffed at him and bonded the first day of her life. She also named herself. The mare seemed to sanction the union. He sure hated that he had had to sell Sniffer's mother so cheap after his wife left him, but she had been too old to come on the trail with the two.

Somewhere between Bell Fourche and the small community of Gillette Wyoming, Randy started really thinking about Salena. He became conscious that he missed her infectious laugh and her beauty as well as all other things about her.

Here he was he thought, attempting to get away from the only good woman he had ever had; by going to the damned ocean just because he hadn't ever seen the thing before. He stopped Sniffer and talked to the horse like she could answer back. Sniffer only twitched her ears and tried to look back to make sure her master was Ok. Randy said. "Now it's August and we're two months away from home if we travel good and steady that is. I reckon we should turn back south and not tackle anymore mountains pard.What do you think about that?"

Sniffer nickered at him and Randy laughed and said, "Well old girl that does it, we go south from Gillette."

He rode into Gillette full of new hope for the future. He bought bacon, flour and some maple syrup for pancakes and lit out south. It was a four day ride to the trading post at Newcastle and his friends Lasiter and Jody. He would love to see them once more.

The Indians came over the rise directly at him and shocked him so bad, that he almost didn't react in time to save his life. The only thing that did save him was his horse Sniffer. When the animal seen the band of fierce looking Sioux warriors coming at her, she turned and fled back the way they had come. Randy and Sniffer had just climbed out of a canyon onto a plain when the Indians attacked them. Almost instantly he was out of the Indians sight.

The band stopped and proceeded with caution. There might be more than one down there. Randy pulled his mount up near an outcropping of rock that afforded him a field of fire back where he could hear unshod horses coming down. He pulled his rifle from its scabbard and grabbed his saddle bags with his ammo inside and leaving Sniffer in the protected little cove, climbed up the cliff a few feet and settled behind a big rock.

He wasn't there more than a minute before the first Indian came in view looking left and right with an arrow notched in his bow. Without hesitation, Randy shot him dead center. As he levered another round in his sharps, another brave appeared and he too bit the dust. Randy shot five before the band realized they were out gunned by these white eyes and pulled back.

One fierce looking brave rode out and shook his spear at him, daring Randy to shoot him. For some reason Randy didn't. He said, "Go away and live another day."

Someone of them must have understood, because that's just what they did. He sat there and watched the band retrieve their dead and retreat back up the draw. He came down and mounted Sniffer and rode like the wind back towards Gillett. He would find another way to Newcastle hopefully without Indians in his way.

The trading post came in view and he hadn't encountered any hostile Indians this time. His friends were happy to see him and put him in one of their spare rooms. He told them what had happened three days ago. Lasiter become excited saying, "So that was you friend. There is much discussion about the many white eyes that killed five brave warriors while not one white eye was killed."

They both had a laugh at that. The rumor had taken flight and would probably fly higher before it was worn out.

One week later Randy was packing his horse to leave when Lasiter said, "There is a delegation of elders from the Sioux tribe here and want to meet with you."

Randy thought, boy I'm in trouble now. He went out with Lasiter to where a group of colorfully dressed Indians sat in a big circle. They all stood as he walked into the circle. He looked at each one in turn and waited for them to talk first. The one with the most elaborate head dress stood and said. "You are brave white man and kill five warriors? Why?"

He sat back down and Randy said. "Because they were going to kill me, that's why."

Randy saw a shock wave go through the elders. They hadn't been told the truth by the young braves. The chief asked how you know this. Randy replied with, "Because they had arrows notched when I shot them."

The Indians rose almost as one and filed away. The Chief said, "Braves not tell truth, thank you."

Lasiter said. "Well, some braves will be set right now Randy and I think you are safe from any Indian attack in the future."

Randy was happy and felt relieved to know Indians had scruples too. He left with the promise that if he ever got back this way he would stop and see them. Jody hugged his neck and said, "Go marry that girl Randy."

Theodore Potter

He looked at her and said, "If she will still have me, I will Jody."

CHAPTER 8
HOMEWARD BOUND

Sniffer was happy to be out on the trail again, they were headed south. Randy had a lot of time to think about his past. He recalled his childhood out in the sand hills of Oklahoma. He had been born into a family that socially skirted on the fringes of the Five Civilized Tribes.

He wasn't enough Indian to be considered a real Indian and this sometime had an adverse effect on life for him and his two siblings. They were looked down on by both races of people as being impure of either blood. For the most part Randy didn't much care and went on his way in spite of the thrown insults of half breed from the white folks and a word from Indians he never learned the meaning of.

He bailed out when he was fifteen, just to get away from an abusive father and a mother that didn't much act like a mother should. His two sisters were older than him and pretty much the chosen ones by his parents. He grew up on a horse and took his pinto pony and rode west. He found himself in northern Texas and warm weather. It had been cold when he reached the end of his tether and left Oklahoma for good.

He rode along the Brazos until it took off up into the Rockies, then rode straight across through the panhandle of Texas into New Mexico, Territory. He found the weather cool at night and warm during the day. It took some searching in order to find a warm cove of some type to sleep in. His little pinto was a great comfort to him and he didn't even have to tie him up at night because he wouldn't leave the campfire.

Randy topped over a hill one evening and run into some punchers sorting cows for branding. Their brand Randy noticed was the Bar S brand. The foreman rode out to intercept him. When he rode up to Randy, he raised his hand in greeting. The man wasn't much older than Randy was. He said, "Howdy, I'm Albert Shipley."

Randy took an instant liking to the boy and answered with, "My name is Randy Mulehouse from Oklahoma."

Albert said, "Come on into our camp and sit down and eat some grub with us. It won't be fancy, but it'll fill the hole up."

Randy had enjoyed the Shipley's so much that he told Albert someday he might come work for them. Albert replied with, I think you might make a good puncher and when you're ready come on back. Randy had ridden away from the Bar S gang with a warm feeling in his breast.

He recalled his trip across the desert southwest to California and the gold fields up in northern California. The disappointment of not striking it big and being robbed of all of the yellow stuff he did find by fly by the night merchants was daunting. These merchants charged four prices for the basic necessities of life.

He stopped mining for the elusive gold and began hanging around town. He thought he had gotten lucky when he met his future wife Romania. It had been a whirl wind of an affair and resulted in them getting married. In all, he had spent three years chasing gold and was tired of it.

When he and Romania tied the knot he thought of the Shipley's ranch and how much he liked them and decided he and his new wife should settle near them. The couple traveled back into the desert southwest once more and stopped near where his ranch is now. He had thought the place would make a good small ranch. He had gone to punching cows for Albert

Shipley. The pay wasn't much, but they were afforded a place to live as well. He had mentioned the land he and Romania had an eye for and Albert had gone to his father Baran Shipley and Baran had filed papers on Randy's behalf at the courthouse in Solana and a deed in Randy's name was given to him with some fan fair one evening. Romania's name had been left off the deed and this bothered her. When Randy approached Albert about that, Albert said, "My wife's name isn't on my deed for this land either Randy. I guess if you want to, you can get her name added at the Court House."

It never came up again before Romania packed up and left for Denver with what was to be her new husband.

CHAPTER 9

Now here he was making a second trip across New Mexico under completely different circumstances.

The brilliant fall colors were spectacular riding across the foothills of the Rockies. The nights were cold at the mile high altitude, but days were warm and sunny. He breezed right on through Denver and didn't even think about stopping and seeing his ex-wife. South of Denver the land went mostly downhill all the way to the Colorado River.

He crossed the river where only a little water flowed. There were pools of water and Sniffer drank her fill. He was really glad to see Trinidad at the border of New Mexico and Colorado. He was out of everything including coffee.

In Trinidad he put Sniffer in the livery and got himself a room with a bed and after visiting the bath house back of the barber shop, fell into bed and slept for twelve full hours. The barber then cut his hair and shaved him, turning him into a decent looking human being once more. There was a restaurant that did a brisk business so he added to their cliental by eating himself half to death with one of the biggest steaks he had ever been served. He left almost half of the thing on his plate and staggered out on the board walk. He needed to walk some of the food off so he went to the livery to check on Sniffer. She was glad to see him and whinnied at him as if to say, "Let's go boss. " He rubbed her nose and told her one more day and then they would head for the Shipley Ranch.

He decided on a beer at the saloon. There was piano music coming out the swinging doors and for once it was in tune. He belled up to the bar and ordered a beer. The bartender was a beefy man with a sour look on his face. The sour look was probably from having to put up with drunks every night. Randy paid his nickel and went to an empty table, hooked a chair with his foot and set down. He noticed the piano player was a handsome girl with raven hair down to her waist. She looked to be about thirty or so. Randy saw that she really felt the music as she played. When she finished the number, Randy clapped his hands. Everyone in the place turned their eyes on him. The girl said, "A music lover at last, thank you kind sir, might you have a request?"

Randy's face grew red and he held both hands palm up and declared he didn't know one song title, but she could choose one for him. She smiled and took off on a rollicking tune Randy had never heard before. He was stomping the floor almost all the way through it. When the lady finished the tune Randy was the only one to clap. Randy felt like the rest should appreciate this piano player too, he stopped clapping and turned to look at the unfriendly staring faces of the town folks. The sour bartender said, "We don't like strangers much in this saloon Mister. finish your beer and leave, and take that hussy of a player with you."

Randy saw red, he stood and walked over to the bar and got right in the bartender's face. He said softly, "Mister you just insulted that lady and if you don't apologize, I will trim your ears right now."

The man reached under the bar for what Randy assumed correctly to be a sawed off shotgun. Randy didn't let him bring it up before he grabbed two hands full of shirt, then placing both feet on the foot rail, heaved the man clean over the bar and onto the floor. He drew his gun at the same time and turned to the others. Two had their guns half drawn when they froze looking down his forty-four barrel. Randy said softly, "Take the hardware out with two fingers and place them on the floor gentleman." He then told them, "Move away from your guns."

He said louder, "If anyone of you holds a hidden gun you better produce it now, because I'll blow the ass off any man who tries to use one on me."

Slowly two more guns of small caliber were brought out and joined the bigger ones. The bartender was frozen in a squatting stance watching him. Randy, motioned him to rise up and he did. Randy said, "Now is when you apologize to the lady Mister."

He stood and waited for the apology. The bartender knew he had been out witted by this stranger and turned to the lady and said. "I'm sorry Mam."

The girl came to Randy and said. "Thank you kind sir, these people don't need anymore music from me."

The two of them backed out of the saloon. On the board walk they were about to descend to the street when Randy heard footsteps running from within, coming to the swinging doors, Randy grabbed the girl and flung her to the side as he pulled leather and confronted the bartender sporting the sawed off shotgun at his shoulder coming through the doors. Randy plugged him twice and he was dead with the first one. His momentum carried him past Randy into the street where he landed in a heap. Randy listened for more footsteps but heard nothing but silence. The girl picked herself up and said, "I owe you a lot Mister, but maybe we should get out of here."

He couldn't agree more. He took her arm and walked swiftly to the livery stable and on the way he swore off saloons forever. He asked the girl where she lived and she pointed, and said, "Down the road a piece."

Sniffer whinnied at him as he grabbed her saddle and blanket, threw them on and cinched them down. His saddle bags were in his room and he would get them later.

When they emerged from the livery there was a small crowd where the bartender lay dead. As the two approached, a marshal appeared and said. You better come to my office. "I've talked to others and it's pretty obvious the man was going to murder you two with that shotgun, so it's only a formality."

They walked to his office down and across the street. In the office the marshal introduced himself as Alfred Potter. He was a circuit US Marshal out of Oklahoma. He had been here for two days and would be on his way shortly. He wanted to know where Randy hailed from and when he found out his ranch bordered the Bar-S; Marshal Potter told him the Shipley's were his friends and that would be his next stop. Randy said, "Well maybe we could ride down together Marshal Potter."

The lady told the two she was scared to stay here in Trinidad for fear of the locals. Maybe she would just pick up stakes and ride with them. They looked at her and Randy asked, "What is your name miss?"

She said, "Elisabeth Palmer. I have played music all the way from New York to here and this is the first time anyone has called me a hussy for it."

They all laughed at that. The Marshal said, "I sure wouldn't mind you two as company on the trail. Get your gear together and meet me back here as soon as you can. I don't think it's healthy to stay here any longer because these folks may turn this deal around and try to take revenge out on you."

The marshal was good company on the trail. He was a bit smitten with Elisabeth and she was attracted to him as well. Soon the two were riding side by side as Randy trailed behind. They camped on a creek that evening and Randy cooked up a turkey he shot. He skinned, gutted and washed the bird then made a spit out of green willow for the meat to roast on. Marshal Potter swore he would starve to death smelling that bird, causing Elisabeth to have a fit of laughter.

After three days the Shipley main house came in view. The Marshal told them he was a friend of the Shipley's and was sure they would make Elisabeth welcome too. Baran and Molly Shipley met them as was their custom out on the front porch. Randy left them to go over to Albert's house. He didn't know the senior Shipley's that well and wanted to talk with Albert anyhow. Randy was welcomed by Albert and they talked into the night. Randy told him what he had been through and now he was going to marry Salena and come back to his ranch. Albert told him he would be re-guarded as a good neighbor.

CHAPTER 10
HOME COMING

The sun was still hot this late November as Randy and Sniffer made the right turn on the trail to the Townsend Ranch. Late that evening he rode up to the house and sat on his horse out front and took the place in. Suddenly the front door burst open and Salena was like a blue streak from the porch to his arms.

She was laughing and crying at the same time. She had lost weight over the summer and seemed as light as a feather. She wouldn't let go of him. Randy saw Joanlea standing on the porch grinning at the two of them. She said, "Boy if you don't think you have been missed around here, you're crazy."

Randy stepped off Sniffer with Salena in his arms and carried her up on the porch. Joanlea hugged the both of them and she had tears in her eyes too. Randy asked Salena if she would be his wife and both women answered yes at the same time. Joanlea said, "She will starve to death if you don't marry her Randy."

The wedding was planned for the first of December and they all went to Yuma to make arrangements. On the big day more people showed up than they thought they knew. The biggest surprise was Roger Shipley came down from fort Apache where he was stationed as a scout for the Army. He had heard from his father and mother there was to be a wedding down here.

Roger wasn't a real Shipley, he was a full blood Apache that had gotten himself wounded in an attack on a wagon train, that Molly and Baran Shipley were moving west with. Roger's real name was Wa-Chee-Bap, this meant little bitty fat boy in Apache. Baran rescued the twelve year old warrior and took the bullet out so he healed up. Roger had taken the way of the white man simply because he owed his life to them. He worshipped both Molly and Baran.

When the wedding was over and everyone went back home, the married couple moved into the foreman's quarters simply because they wanted some days alone together. Joanlea understood and left them alone.

A few days later they were sated and came to the house to talk with Joanlea about the other ranch. Joanlea listened to them and then said. "That ranch needs money to make it pay off and this one doesn't. Now if you want to go up there and work your butts off for nothing, I'll let you. You are both old enough to make any decision you want to, but let me say this to you Randy; this ranch belongs to you now as much as it does to my daughter and me. I can't run this place by myself and I need the both of you to help. I am willing to put in writing how I think the profits can be shared three ways. Would that interest you Randy?"

Randy had a glazed look in his eyes, because he hadn't even thought that way. He looked at his beautiful wife and said, "Ok by me if it's ok by you sweetheart."

Salena jumped in his arms and exclaimed. "That it was a wonderful plan"

Joanlea said. "You can live here until a bigger place can be built. You two take over the east wing and we'll share the kitchen and living areas."

The next few weeks were busy ones for Randy. He had to be briefed on the internal operations of a ranch that grossed a hundred thousand dollars plus per year. The amount of work that went in to raising horses was somewhat less than a cow ranch would take. For one thing there was nothing dumber than a cow;

while a horse was just smart enough to hurt you, especially if you were unaware around them. Randy loved horses and it transmitted to the herd and anytime he went to the corrals he always had a crowd of horses around him. He almost got hurt one time because of their exuberance. He was hemmed up in a bad place while warding off excited horses. He began keeping fences between him and the bunch as he laughingly called them. For the most part the horses made more horses with only a few directions from the ranch personnel that prevented interbreeding and incest.

The herd consisted of two hundred brood mares and four stallions to service them. Two times a year the young were taken to Yuma and Tucson. The Army bought ninety percent of their product and the rest were turned into brood mares with new studs so that the ranch saw a solid ten percent growth annually.

Randy wanted to know where their feed came from and was told it came from the valley the other side of Yuma. It came each fall in a huge wagon train of up to twenty wagons piled thirty feet high with hay.

Only a small percentage of the range could be used to raise livestock because of the lack of water out in the desert. The Gila River didn't always flow above ground, but there was ample water below ground. There had to be holes dug for watering spots along the sandy bed. After each rain, that only happened infrequently, the holes had to be re dug again. Randy always wondered if there was some way to get the water up to the fields, so they could grow crops out here. He racked his brain, but came up with nothing.

He did hear rumors that a thing called a pump had been invented that with a wind mill for power, pumped water out of the ground and into a tank nearby. That would be the thing to have. He told Joanlea he wanted to go somewhere and find out about the new windmill. She sanctioned him and Salena going back east on a fact finding trip.

CHAPTER 11

There was a road of sorts wherever Randy and Salena traveled in their rig, but most had ruts so deep he was afraid the horse would break a leg. Randy took to going cross country more and more. He and Salena were in eastern Kansas near the Missouri border.

They had left the ranch in Arizona in a brand new buggy that Randy had designed himself. From his days of being on the trail he had learned one thing. The elements were your worst enemy. With that in mind, he had taken a stretched out buggy made for a cargo buggy and turned it into a place to sleep out of the weather. It was canvas covered and looked strangely out of place, but it could rain like hell and the occupants would stay warm and dry. Only one horse pulled the rig too, so Old Sniffer had to trail behind. Sometime Randy saddled her and rode along while Salena drove the rig. They had great fun doing this. They were always calling back and forth to one another. When they camped at night Randy took care that they camped in a spot that could be defended and water was near.

On one of their camp sites, two riders approached the strange wagon slowly. They were on the make for anything that would enhance their living style and this wagon looked like easy pickings. Randy said. "Hold it right there boys. We really don't need company, but if I can help you in any way just sing out."

Both men stopped their advance on the wagon and one said, "Sorry friend we didn't mean any harm."

The two then wheeled around and left the way they came. Randy told Salena to pack up things. He didn't trust those two and would rather fight them on the run rather than in this closed up place. Within five minutes they were on their way. Randy riding Sniffer and Salena was driving the buckboard.

Randy hung back a hundred feet and saw the attack coming off from the left. He wheeled Sniffer to the left and within ten leaps was flanking the two outlaws. Randy shot the first one just as he was trying to draw a bead on his wife. The one in the rear saw his mate pitch out of the saddle and looked over at Randy who was on full tilt charge. He started to bring his six gun up and Randy blew him right out of the saddle with a well-placed shot. The outlaw died with a surprised look on his face.

Randy didn't even slow down because he knew his wife would be some kind of shook up by now. He came up on the wagon and Salena leaped from the spring seat into his arms and clung on for dear life. Sniffer shied sideways for a bit and then settled down. Salena was softly crying. She said, "Those men were out to murder us weren't they Randy?"

Randy held her tight and said. "They sure were and would have if we hadn't outsmarted them baby."

CHAPTER 12

The contraption looked strange to Randy. There was a long cylinder with a ram rod in it and a thing called a crank shaft that moved the ram rod up and down when the wind turned the blades of the wind mill. Water then flowed out a nozzle into a wash tub, only to repeat the process over and over. There was a placard on the frame that gave a brief history of the windmill. It had been invented back in the 500's by a Dutchman. It was being sold to every farmer rancher east of the Mississippi and now was available through the Randle Mill Company. It came with a set of instructions even an idiot could follow.

The two were at the Philadelphia trade fair on a Saturday afternoon in the month of June. Their trip across two thousand miles of North America was only marred by the two outlaws Randy had had to kill in Arkansas. It had taken thirty-eight days to make the trip, but from what Randy saw it was going to be worth it. This new old machine could well be the answer to what their water problem was out west. The specifications said the pump would draw water from sixty feet underground and if they dug wells next to the river at home they wouldn't exceed ten feet.

CHAPTER 13

They began their return trip on the last day of June 1856. The weather was balmy and spring like. Near ST. Louis, Salena began having a hard time keeping food down. At first they passed it off as maybe some bad food at one of the eating places they ate at along the way, but as the day passed, she became more and more ill until Randy went looking for and found a doctor in East ST Louis, on the Illinois side.

The doctor took one look and quarantined the both of them. He recognized cholera the minute he saw it. There was not any medicine available to fight the fever with except cold compresses on the victims face and body. Randy wasn't affected by the bug, but Salena was so hot that she was cooking in her own juices. Randy was put to work keeping her cool. The doctor told him that was their only hope. For two days and nights he kept her alive, and then she looked at him and said weakly, "I'm sorry sweetheart I can't make it. Please take me home after I'm gone."

She closed her eyes and died in his arms. He stayed with her all that night crying his heart out. Morning came and the doctor pulled him away from the body and led him away.

In another room Randy told him of her last request. The doctor shook his head and told him that was next to impossible this time of year and besides the body was carrying the Cholera bug and must be buried today in order to keep an epidemic from taking place.

Randy knew he was right, but it broke his heart that he couldn't honor his lover's last request. They put her in the ground in a nice little cemetery near a park in East St Louis. Randy had a hard time walking away from the grave.

He finally returned to the doctor's office and squared up with him and the mortician. He drove the buggy out to a place along the Mississippi River and after turning the horse into a pack mule pushed the buggy over the bluff and watched it bounce once and then fly through the air and hit the waters of the River and disappear.

He stood with sadness permeating his very soul. He was really alone for the first time in his life. Sniffer sensed his loneliness and nickered softly at him. Randy went to the mare and put his arms around her neck and cried some more.

Sniffer stood perfectly still for him. Finally he swung up on her back and headed west once more. Those next few days he would start to say something to Salena and have to catch himself and the pain of her departure would began all over again and he would relive the last few days.

CHAPTER 14

The town of Salina New Mexican Territory came in sight and he saw that it had grown since he had left it. He rode to the Sheriff's office and swung down. He went in and found a much older law officer there. He couldn't believe he had been gone that long. The man smiled at Randy and asked what he could do for him. Randy realized then that this wasn't the same sheriff as before. Randy said "You must be new here sir."

The sheriff laughed and said. "Well you must be thinking of Ezera Blankenship then, he bought a small ranch out of town a half days ride east of here and retired. He is raising enough cows to keep him and his misses in food and things. He comes into town often."

Randy asked him the directions to the small ranch and was shocked that the directions led him straight to his old place. He exclaimed, "That's my old place."

The new sheriff said, "Well if that's so, you better check your bank balance over at the bank here in town young feller, because old Ezera paid you for that ranch, I know that for a fact."

The banker said, "So you're the one that left the ranch for Ezra to sell for you, well, let me tell you he bought it himself and paid you a handsome price for it son."

The banker wrote some numbers on a note pad and ripped it off and handed it to Randy. There was the goodly sum of $2,947.00 in his name in this bank. Randy was astounded that all this time he had been rich and didn't know it. He asked the banker for all of it. He explained he didn't live near here any longer and would deposit the money in another bank somewhere.

CHAPTER 15

Randy Mulehouse knew mortal fear for the first time in his life. He couldn't bring himself to face Joanlea directly and tell her he had failed to keep her only daughter safe from harm. He anguished about it for days until finally he sat himself down and wrote her a letter. He cried on the pages, but knew this was the only way out for him and he would disappear somewhere and never set foot near that ranch again.

Bill stopped his horse and took in the ranch and the house. He thought his sister Joanlea had done a marvelous job with the place. He had picked up a letter from Randy in Tucson and he had a bad feeling about its contents. He had decided he would deliver it in person, rather than put it in the box on the trail. He found Joanlea watering her flowers along the front path. He said, "Hey sis got a letter for you from Randy and Salena."

Joanlea ripped it out of Tom's hand and opened it by tearing the end off. She read the lines Randy wrote and with a scream fell to the ground. Bill ran to her aid, but saw she was out cold.

He picked the letter up and read it. He sat down on the grass and put his head in his hands. He kept thinking this is unreal; his favorite niece had died from cholera way out in the middle of nowhere. Randy was afraid to come home and face them about it. He hurt for Randy too. The boy somehow thought he was responsible for Salena's death.

Joanlea came around and grabbed her brother and sobbed her heart out. Bill was at a loss as how to console his sister and was in almost as bad of a shape as his sister was.

CHAPTER 16

Randy Earl Mulehouse became a recluse. His only contact with humans was when he had to buy supplies. He had traveled to the Rocky Mountains and lost himself in them by only traveling short distances at a time. The trails he mostly rode over were game trails. He came up on many animals that traveled these tracks and if it was editable and he needed meat he shot the thing. One time he and Sniffer got some excitement when they came up on a huge Grizzly Bear. The thing reared up to its full ten foot height and bellowed loud enough to scare both horse and man half to death. Sniffer squealed and didn't need much encouragement to run like hell back down the trail. The Grizzly pursued them for a few hundred feet than gave up. Old Sniffer wasn't about to be caught by any bear.

Randy looked for campsites that could be easily defended. Caves were many and most offered some cover out front and provided cover from rains and insects. One day he found a veritable paradise. He came up on a water fall and a pool that was thirty foot across. The water fell a hundred feet to the pool. There was a rainbow across the pool when the sun was just right.

Somehow he thought of the place as Salena's pool and water fall. It seemed to give him solace of some kind, just to set on the rocky edge of the pool and remember the wonderful woman he had lost. He hoped Joanlea hadn't thought too badly of him for not facing up to his responsibilities. Maybe someday he could face her, but not right now.

He heard something at the mouth of his cave and it sent a chill up his back. He'd heard that noise once before up in Spearfish Canyon some years ago. He had cat for company. Sniffer was staked out where she could reach water and hadn't been disturbed by the cat. Suddenly he was hit by such a force it took his breath away. He had just gotten his six gun in his hand when the cat jumped on him. They both went down and Randy could feel pain from its claws. With great difficulty he brought the gun around and put the muzzle against the animal's neck and pulled the trigger.

The mountain lion fell limp and heavy on him. Randy rolled the big cat off him and staggered to his feet. He was hurt, but couldn't tell how bad in the pitch dark. He lit a match and found some kindling and grass and then lit a fire.

His left arm seemed to have more damage than the rest of his body. He realized then he had been bitten by the cat below the elbow. His arm was mangled to shreds and he had to stop the bleeding somehow. He grabbed his pigging string off his saddle and wound the hide string tightly around the arm above the elbow. The bleeding slowed and he inspected his arm closer. There were bite marks and one long rip in his flesh of his lower arm. He held the rip together and wrapped the pigging string around it. His main injury was his left arm and that was pretty bad. He made bandages out of one of his clean shirts and wrapped the entire mess up and bound it with strips of a blanket. He saw a few scratches where the cat had raked him with his claws but no deep ones. By the time he got the bleeding stopped it was growing light in the east.

He saddled Sniffer and turned his other horse loose to follow along if it wanted and pointed Sniffer east down the mountain. Sniffer seemed to know time was Randy's enemy and when they reached the main trail down to Denver she laid her ears back and without any encouragement from Randy ran her heart out.

When they reached the outskirts of Denver Randy was more dead than alive. Sniffer was wet with sweat and Randy's blood. Her superb condition was the only reason she made it. Randy went straight to the Marshal's office. He more or less fell out of his saddle onto the ground.

A woman walking down the board walk screamed when she saw all the blood. People seemed to appear out of every door then. Hands took hold of him and he could only let them bare him along. He heard the word doctor and other words that meant he was being taken care of so he went to sleep after saying, "Take care of my horse please."

Randy became conscious by degrees. He first was aware that he was in a clean bed and there was a window on his left. The light was too bright for his eyes at first, then he began hearing other sounds. They suggested it was meal time where ever he was. He smelled food and was surprised that he was starved. A nurse came near and peered at him and exclaimed, "You've awoke sir, how do you feel?"

Randy said, "Hungry."

She laughed and replied with, "Well, I think you just might be Ok then."

Randy looked down at his wounded arm and saw it was neatly bandaged. It felt sore as hell however and he wouldn't be riding through the mountains anytime too soon. He had bandages all over his front and each one was a sore spot. A doctor came in and smiled at him. "Good morning sir, how do you feel today?"

Randy decided he had better not be a wise ass with this man and told him the truth. "I hurt all over doctor."

The doctor replied with, "I shouldn't wonder, you expended all of our supply of alcohol to disinfect what looked like a meat grinder's deed. That must have been some big cat to tear you up this bad. We're hoping for no infection because that might mean we would have to amputate your arm."

Randy looked at the doctor long and hard then said. "If I can't have all my parts doc I'll die with them still attached, thank you sir."

No infection set in and Randy was released three days later with a warning, that he should not attempt bandaging himself, but come back to the hospital on a daily basis and let his nurse do the job right. Randy agreed and went to find his horse. The livery was only down the street, but Randy was plumb worn out by the time he walked there. He sat down on a chair at the street entrance to the stables and rested. He had lost so much blood and it would take time to rebuild his strength. He found Sniffer in the corral out back. Sniffer whinnied and ran over to him and nuzzled his good arm. He was glad to see his horse and know she hadn't been hurt by his mad run to town.

Randy heard someone behind him and turned to confront a young woman about his age. She smiled and introduced herself as Delfye Jameson, the roustabout here at the stable. Delfye was a bright blue eyed lass with freckles on her nose and a semi-permanent smile on her face. Her voice sounded like the wind blowing through a pass in the mountains. She was dressed like a man from the neck down and wore a six shooter tied down to her leg. A set of chaps and boots with spurs completed the outfit.

Randy realized with a jolt, that he was looking at his first cowgirl in a long time and he liked what he saw. Delfye said. "You were in pretty bad shape when my mother first saw you on the street the other day sir."

Randy told her. "You don't need to call me sir, my name is Randy Earl Mulehouse and I'm glad to meet you."

She said. "Same here and I have your saddle bags over at our place. My father is the marshal here in town and was one of the men that dragged your almost dead carcass over to our small hospital. Man, they used so much alcohol on you, that the whole town smelled of it. The nurse is my aunty and told me you have more than a hundred stitches all over your body. You must be some kind of sore Randy."

She finally run down and let Randy get a word in edge wise. He said. "Thanks for looking after my horse."

Delfye reddened and looked at the toes of her boots, then said. "That is one hell of a piece of horse flesh Randy. I think she could have made it another ten miles and still be ok."

Randy thought, maybe he liked this girl.

CHAPTER 17

Bill had heard that Randy came here to Denver from time to time to buy supplies. He needed to find this boy and set him straight about things. Down at the Marshal's office he was welcomed and told all about Randy being attacked by a mountain lion.

Bill noticed the young girl got red in the face when Randy's name was mentioned. Bill thought girl, you better give that boy a lot of time before you stake your claim. He wasn't ready to turn loose of Salena yet and may never in fact. She told Bill that she didn't know exactly where Randy called home these days, but it wasn't too far from here and she could probably lead him up there and find him if he wanted. Bill was tempted, but it might mean to Randy that he sanctioned a union between this veracious girl and Randy. Old Bill didn't want to interfere in anyway. He made his excuses and left. He rode west out of Denver.

He had some idea about where Randy might seclude himself and would follow his nose. He didn't realize it, but the girl wasn't far behind him. She knew these hills better than Bill did and might have to point him in the right direction, discreetly of course.

Randy had told her about the love of his life dying in his arms of Cholera two years before. She understood he needed time and cared enough for him to give it to him. He needed to return and face his past however and Bill was the link that was needed for that to happen.

She rode ahead of Bill that night and began searching for a trail Randy had mentioned and when she found it she made sure there were plenty of tracks leading up in the mountains. She then rode ahead some mile or so and went to sleep close to her horse. Morning came and she moved off the trail some and waited to make sure her bait had been taken. She didn't realize that old Bill figured out what she was up to when he saw all the tracks. He chuckled and said out loud, "You hang in there girl, maybe someday you'll be what this wayward boy really needs.

Bill rode all that day along traveled game trails. He saw Randy's old tracks from time to time. He came in sight of one of the most beautiful water falls he had ever seen. There was a beautiful blue pool of water where it disappeared. He froze when a voice said, "Mister put your hands in the air and grab some sky."

Bill's hands shot up and the voice went on, "What do you want here Mister?"

Bill said, "I'm looking for a boy that didn't do a thing wrong and never came home to some folks that love him like a son, after the tragic death of his wife."

Randy had tears to suddenly spring to his eyes and course down his cheeks. He holstered his gun and went to Bill. Bill dismounted and hugged Randy. He said, "Son, Joanlea has been going downhill fast. Not only did she lose a daughter, she lost a son as well. You need to come home long enough to give her some closure over her daughter's death son.

There is a girl on my trail that admires you very much and I think she will always do so. She needs something to hang on to as well."

Randy nodded his head and went to put his gear together. The pack horse had stayed right here and ran to them when he and Sniffer had ridden in. He packed all he wanted to take with him and as he led the pack horse out, Delfye rode in camp and looked at Bill sheepishly. Bill said, "Well imagine this. A cowgirl way out here in the mountain's. I guess you two know each other after all."

Randy said. "This is Delfye and she looked after my horse after I damn near killed the poor thing, after a lion grabbed me in the dark. I was dumb enough to not have a fire or that would never have happened."

CHAPTER 18

Bill, Delfye and Randy rode to Denver then Bill and Randy turned south and parted company with Delfye. She had tears in her eyes when Randy hugged her goodbye and told her he would be back as soon as possible. She thought she might never see him again, but her heart sang when Bill winked at her and nodded his head.

Randy still had a heavy heart knowing he had to face Joanlea about Salena dying on the track, but he also knew his friend Bill was right and besides Bill had gone to a great deal of trouble to find him.

When the ranch came in sight eight days later Randy had mustered up the courage to face Joanlea. He was still unprepared by what took place. Joanlea came out of the house and stood there looking at him with tears streaming down her face. When Randy dismounted she flew into his arms. She bawled for thirty minutes. Randy had tears flowing and Bill was openly crying. Joanlea drug him into the house. She held him at arm's length and stamped her right foot and said, "This is your home son and don't you ever think it's not, ever again."

CHAPTER 19

Randy rode Sniffer down the main street of Denver showing off her brand new Mexican saddle Joanlea had given him for his twenty-seventh birthday. He left the ranch a few days after he celebrated it on the twenty-third of June. He and Joanlea had talked all winter about everything. Randy told her about Delfye up in Denver and Joanlea had a moment of thinking, but what about Salena, then caught herself and broke out in tears. She told Randy that Delfye sounded like a wonderful person and she would be welcomed here anytime.

Now after seven months he had made his way back to Denver. He stopped off at the marshal's office, dismounted and went in. There was a stranger sitting in the marshal's chair. He was a young brash man not much older than eighteen years. Randy asked where he might find the marshal these days and the brash kid came back with, out at his farm at the edge of town. I go with his daughter Delfye and if you want I'll ride out with you and show you their place. Randy's heart felt like lead for just a moment before he realized this young whippersnapper was full of it and the girl he knew wouldn't look at him twice. He held up his hand and said, "No thanks I can find my way there I believe."

He turned and walked out leaving the smart ass with his mouth hanging open. He remounted Sniffer and road east out of town. The land turned to grasslands at this point. He read mail boxes and when he saw Jameson painted on one he turned down that road. He walked Sniffer and took in the neat farm, as he approached. He saw her before she saw him, but Sniffer gave the game away by calling out to someone he liked with a whinny. Delfye's head snapped up and when her eyes focused on him, she dropped whatever she had in her hands and at a dead run she came to him.

The wedding was held in Denver that Saturday and would be held again at the ranch in Arizona when they got there. Randy and his new bride decided to spend their honeymoon at the waterfall. The parents wanted them to stay in Denver and live, but when Randy explained that he was part owner in a million acre horse ranch in Arizona they understood. The brash new marshal came to the wedding and told Randy he was sorry he had spoken out of turn and had meant to say he only wished he and Delfye were going together. The married couple had a good laugh at that. The two bought enough food and a canvas tent big enough to set up housekeeping in and packed it all on the two spare horses. Sniffer looked at the two high packed horses and snorted at Randy. They rode out of Denver headed west on a warm late spring day. The birds were singing and their hearts were filled with more hope than ever before.

Randy still had bad moments when Salena would cross his mind briefly and he would experience a sadness that never quite went away, but he couldn't stay sad around this bubbly girl. She knew how he felt even when he didn't and always seemed to be there to lift him up from the doldrums, when they happened.

The falls and pool were even more beautiful to the two than they remembered. Randy picked an open area to pitch their tent. Some poles had to be cut; as the tent wasn't a free standing one. Randy took the bow saw he had purchased in Denver and cut them from a stand of lodge pole pine not far from camp. Delfye was a go getter and soon had the tent looking like a home in the forest. They both lay in enough dry firewood to last several nights. They then went to bed and consummated their marriage.

Randy couldn't get over how different Delfye was from his previous wife. At first he tried in his mind to compare Delfye to Salena and that just didn't work. There was no comparison between the two, so he gave up trying and just enjoyed the sweetness in this girl. She turned out to be a great cook as well and began fattening him up once more. He had never gained the weight back he lost after the mountain lion tore his body to pieces, but she was taking care of that now.

Randy killed an elk and dressed it out for meat. There was still some snow in a few places and he found one drift that was almost ten feet deep. He dug a tunnel to the center of the bank and stashed their meat supply in it. The two would spend the summer here and the winters down in the Mohave Desert working the ranch.

CHAPTER 20

Joanlea wasn't too sure she liked the idea of Randy bringing a new wife home that replaced her dead but not forgotten daughter, but the moment the new girl dismounted her horse and walked with Randy to the front porch and Joanlea saw the smiling girl, she lost all her reserve and flew to her and Randy and hugged and cried with them both. Randy moved back a step and let the two women cry in each other's arms. He saw someone coming up the walk and recognized his old friend Bill. The two men shook hands and pummeled each other on the back. Joanlea said, "Bill lives out here now that he retired from Wells Fargo."

Randy said, "I was going to suggest that when I got back, welcome to the ranch Bill."

Bill said good naturedly, that someone had to look after the place when he went gallivanting around the country.

Randy said, "If I didn't escape the summer heat down here I would shrivel up and die."

Bill said, "I was like that in my younger days, but now, the heat feels good in my old bones."

They all laughed and moved inside, the weather was still hot here in the month of October. All in all Randy thought the homecoming was a success.

Randy noticed that Joanlea had aged a great deal and looked poorly. He talked to Bill about her one day. Bill said. "Yeah we all get old and die and there's not a thing we can do about it."

Randy said, "I think she might be sick with something and not doing anything about it."

Bill was thoughtful for a while then said. "You know, you may have something there, I've noticed she is not eating like normal and sits around a lot."

Randy's heart froze as he remembered his lovely wife dying in such a short time after becoming sick. He decided to speak directly to Joanlea about it. He went where she was darning some socks in the living room and sat near her on a soft chair. They made small talk for some time and then Randy asked her point blank if she was feeling well. Joanlea froze and closed her eyes. She whispered softly, "I've tried my best to hide it son. I have pain in my left chest and I'm tired all the time. I just don't have any energy to do anything."

Randy went to her and said, "Get yourself ready, we're going to Denver where they have good doctors, and I'll not take no for an answer either."

Joanlea looked at him with big eyes and said, "Do you really think that's necessary son?"

Randy said, "It is and I don't mean later, I mean now. You, I and Delfye will take a buggy and two horses and go there; Bill can take care of things here."

Joanlea knew Randy was right and went and packed. Randy found his wife with old Bill. He found them out repairing some railings that had been knocked down along the walkway. When he told them what was happening, Delfye ran to Joanlea and hugged her and told her it would be alright.

The three of them were on the road to Denver before an hour was up. A pallet was made for Joanlea in case she got tired and needed to lie down. Randy rode Sniffer and there was a spare saddled horse trudging along behind the buggy. Delfye drove the buggy at a fast clip that ate the miles up. When dark over took them, Joanlea stretched out in the bed of the buggy while the Millhouse's pitched their bedrolls on the ground and went to sleep. Randy had the buggy hooked up and both horses saddled up by first light. They would make it into

New Mexico today and Colorado by day after tomorrow.

It was a long way to Denver, but Denver had the only decent hospital around and Randy suspected that Joanlea might just die unless she received some excellent medical care. The lady in question was holding her own and she was happy to be going anyhow. Maybe that was what was wrong with her; she had worried herself sick over her daughter's death and then the disappearance of Randy, while he was broken hearted. The way she thought of it was; all she had gone through was enough to kill anyone. She began to feel better the third day. Randy was tickled that his medicine was working.

The colors were spectacular in the hills of aspens through Colorado foot hills. Near Denver it spit snow on them and then the sun came out and it warmed up. They were just in time because a snow storm could come at any time. They pulled into Denver hospital just at dark. Joanlea was more tired than she let on and her complexion was darker than ever. The Nurse, {Delfye's aunty} took one look at Joanlea and put her on a gurney and wheeled her to emergency. The doctor looked at her and thought, heart. Give her some laudanum for pain and let's get her on some of that new stuff for chest pain. The nurse said with a smile, "Do you mean nitro pills doctor?"

The doctor threw his hands up and said good natured, "I wonder who the doctor is here?"

Even Joanlea laughed at his funny remark.

The doctor said, "Mam, you have heart failure, the thing is as big as a cantaloupe and won't ever work right again. Your life can be made better, but you will never be able to return to working."

Joanlea was devastated and cried. Delfye and Randy were there to console her, but she still felt like she had been cheated out of the rest of her life. She was fifty-nine years old and had been active her entire life. The doctor tried to explain congestive heart failure to her. All Joanlea wanted was to be well enough to go home. The doctor said, "You will die there with no medical help near."

Joanlea asked, "Will I not die right here as well doctor?"

The doctor's face reddened and he stuttered a bit and then said, "You are right Mrs. Townsend, and I have no right trying to convince you to stay here. I can give you some things to help you through some of your pain, but taking it easy is the most important thing of all."

They went south the next day just to outrun the first snow to dump on Denver that fall. Randy chose to go straight south and cross over the southern route to Arizona. They were very close to the Shipley's ranch but it was fall round up and everyone would be busy. The return trip was much slower than going up. The main consideration was that Joanlea become tired much quicker now because she had to look at everything along the way instead of resting more.

In Gila Bend, they stopped and installed Joanlea in Bills house. She was too tired to continue the trip home. Bill hadn't lived here for a long time, but someone kept the place clean for him. There wasn't much of a market for a converted stable; if there had been, Bill would have sold the place long ago.

After making Joanlea as comfortable as possible, Randy and Delfye went to the only eating place in town and had some food. They took some back to Joanlea and found her hungry and wanting to talk to them. Joanlea told them to sit down and listen to her as she considered what she had to say was important. She said. "I soon will be sixty years old and now that I know I have a bad ticker. I think we need to talk about the ranch. I don't feel I will last much longer. The ranch will become yours upon my death. The only stipulation is my brother Bill may finish out his day's there on the place with you. Do you agree with that?"

Both Randy and Delfye nodded their head at her. Joanlea added "I have grown fond of both of you even though you're not of my blood and consider you my children. There is a considerable amount of money in the bank as you know and that becomes yours as well. Now why don't you let me get some rest so we can go home tomorrow?"

Randy and Delfye hugged the frail woman before they left the room, both had tears in their eyes. Randy didn't really know what to say. He wished Joanlea would live on because he loved the Rocky Mountains and in particular the falls and pool he considered now to be his and Delfye's. He thought maybe he would sell the ranch or give it to Bill; he'd have to give that some serious thought.

CHAPTER 21

How much did you say? Randy couldn't even count that high. The banker said patently once again seven hundred thousand seven hundred and thirty dollars and thirteen cents. Randy was near fainting and was holding on to Delfye for support. His mother in law had died leaving them a fortune. He couldn't speak for a time. He thought back two months to the trip from Gila Bend home.

It had been slow because Joanlea worsened on them and Delfye had to hold her head and cool her brow with water all the way. When they put her to bed in her room she faintly asked for her brother Bill. Bill talked to his only sister for fifteen minutes and came out crying. Delfye went to him and hugged him; the old fellow was devastated, his younger sister was dying on him. He said, "I thought surely she would plant me and now I have to bury my only living relative. Bill said She explained her wishes and I agree I don't need much to keep me anymore and you two have your entire life before you."

Sadness had descended on the ranch and even the hired hands went about the place quietly, almost as if, they thought that if they were quiet, Joanlea might have a sudden reversal of her condition.

Thirty seven days later, they all heard a scream and rushed to Joanlea's room. The Mexican nurse that attended her was weeping and wringing her hands. The grand lady had lost her battle for life and was lying with open unseeing eyes in her bed.

It had been hard on everyone when Joanlea was laid to rest beside her husband in the small graveyard that now had two graves resting in it.

Now Randy was sitting with his wife in the bank in Yuma being told he was a rich man and still owned a million acre horse ranch in a fertile valley in the middle of Arizona. The two of them walked out into the bright sunshine and climbed up in the seat of their buggy. Both sat and had pretty much the same thought. Joanlea had been a wonderful woman and would always be remembered by them.

CHAPTER 22

"What did you say boy?"

Randy repeated himself, "We want you to have the ranch and all the stock, You can take the crew and drive a herd to Yuma, that'll give you operating capitol aplenty and me and my wife want to live in the Rocky Mountains west of Denver. You are long in the tooth old friend and if it's too much for you; you can always sell or desert the place, it's your choice. You are welcome at our place that we will build this summer if you don't want to stay here."

Bill shook his head and replied. "I thought that's what you said son. Let me think about this for a bit."

Bill finally said. "I don't want to stay here without you two being here too. So my answer is no, I want to go to your mountains with you and build myself a little cabin and stay cool for the rest of my life."

Randy and Delfye got tickled at him and Randy spoke, "We will just sell the stock and we all shall move our butts to the mountains then, is that alright Bill?"

The herd was the biggest Randy had ever driven. They had counted over three thousand head the day before. Randy put the mares out front so the others would follow without scattering everywhere. The drive went smooth and the army as always was only too happy to buy every last one. Randy had shot them a price of six dollars a head. This was half of the market price for horses, but unloading three thousand head all at once made it hard to get that price.

He took cash and didn't need to touch the bank money. He paid all the punchers off and told them so long. One Mexican with a wife and two sons was hired as caretakers and told he could farm and raise stock if they wanted. The big house was boarded up and the family had the foreman's house and the bunk house to live in. Randy made the Mexicans understand he and Delfye would be down from time to time to make sure everything was ok.

Randy, Delfye and old Bill packed two wagons and a buggy with more than they were supposed to haul and headed east. It was early June and Randy wanted to cross the great divide before July. He turned northeast at Gila Bend. The high desert near fort flagstaff was cool all summer. The great divide was on the Brigham young trail to Salt Lake. When they picked it up after flagstaff it would be downhill to Durango. After Durango they went straight to the big springs a hundred miles south of Denver.

CHAPTER 23

Denver yielded more tools and gear than Randy first thought it would. The only tool he couldn't find was a two man cross cut saw and there wasn't one to be bought in Denver. He was about to order the thing when Delfye piped up and said, "My father has one of those things hanging in the shed at home."

The retired marshal was only too happy to throw the saw at them with some words to the effect that he wasn't about to come out of retirement to use it anyhow. Later he would eat those words. Randy bought two more pack horses and another tent for Bill.

They left Denver on a sunny morning in June and inched their way to the falls above Denver.

The place was perfect for what Randy had in mind. There was a hill side that was facing south overlooking the falls and pool and that's where he wanted to build a lodge that he and Delfye could be proud of.

Randy knew he wasn't any kind of a carpenter at his maddest moment, so he had contacted a fellow who built log dwellings back in Denver by the name of Robert Neilson. He contracted him to build the log structure when he finished the house he was building now.

All Randy, Bill and Delfye had to do was cut, haul and skin building logs down to the lodge site. Randy had purchased a single tree and harness for a horse that would hook up to a good sized log to be pulled down the mountain. Bill and Randy were the saw men and Delfye rode the harnessed horse and towed logs down the mountain one at a time.

The stand of lodge pine Randy chose was a beautiful stand of timber. Randy didn't clear cut the stand but left younger trees to grow into bigger ones. They cut and trimmed for three days. There were more than enough logs to build the lodge with some left over for Bill's cabin. Bill and Randy took turns on the peeling spud, but still wound up with blisters on their hands in spite of the gloves they wore. After five days Randy called a day of rest and healing.

Delfye had a sore bottom from riding the horse from day light till dark and flat refused to get on the dad burn thing again. Of course she would if she had too, but all the logs were off the mountain now.

Randy and Bill laughed at the funny way Delfye said it. Bill had gone out the day before and killed a fat elk not a mile from camp. He came in with it across his horse and him walking. Randy and Delfye was amazed that Bill was able to get the thing on his horse. Bill explained that he had used the horse and lariat to haul the dressed elk up a tree limb and after tying the rope off, he simply backed the horse under the elk and let it down on the horse.

According to Bill the hardest thing was that the horse didn't much like having a dead animal on his back, so Bill used his rope to tie the elk in place so the crazed horse couldn't buck it off. The way Bill told this story made Delfye and Randy so tickled they were on the ground they laughed so hard. Randy was sure glad Bill was here.

The elk meat was delicious the way Delfye cooked it up. Delfye had bought cooking gear and spices back in Denver. Whatever spice she added to the elk sure made it taste good enough that the two men swore to imprison Delfye and make her cook only.

Randy and Delfye rode to town and made contact with their builder Robert Neilson. He was near finished with his project and would come to the falls with his two sons and camp until the lodge was completed. Robert knew where the falls were because he and his sons hunted out there each fall.

Randy made a list of Robert's needs and went on a buying spree. Window glass was the heavy stuff and had to be divided between two pack horses. Delfye had been adamant that there would be windows galore on the south facing front wall. Randy didn't argue he just bought the window glass. Robert told him he could build them in as the lodge went up. Other windows that opened up for fresh air could be installed at a later date. Doors were a problem but Robert assured them he could make doors that would be bullet proof and Randy believed him.

The trip back out was slow and tedious. The box's holding the glass seemed to catch on everything. Randy was working his tail off with a machete clearing a way for the over width horses. Two times he had to go around the old trail and make a new one. This meant delay after delay and they didn't get home until full dark.

Bill met them with a lantern glowing. Randy shuddered to think about trying to unload four horses in the dark. The glass made the trip without breaking any panes. Delfye was amazed they made it without the stuff falling off a horse.

When morning came they all were amazed that all that gear had come from just four horses.

CHAPTER 24

Robert and his two sons arrived two days later. The two strapping lads were Donald and his younger brother Joseph. They were friendly and courteous. Both grew red when introduced to Delfye and stared at the toes of their scuffed boots. It tickled all the others. Soon they lost their shyness and went to work on the logs.

Randy and Bill had dug back into the hillside for thirty feet or so and using the horse had pulled good sized rocks down from the hill and lined the back wall with them. The slope was no more than ten degrees and when they got finished they had created a pad of mostly rock thirty by forty feet with a south view of the falls and pool that was absolutely spectacular. Robert exclaimed that he thought this was the most beautiful home site in Colorado.

The very first day, the base logs were laid in and locked together. Delfye and Randy couldn't keep their eyes off it. Day two found Robert using an adz to flatten each log after it was laid in the floor. Randy watched and marveled at how simple Robert made it look. He and Bill helped as much as possible, but this consisted mostly of clearing away cuttings and lifting logs for Robert when he needed to re cut a notch.

Robert had them to bring up rock to build a fire place with. He had left a large dent at the east end for that purpose. One of the sons would cut and lay the stones so well fitted together that no smoke would escape through the cracks. The house slowly took shape as the days then weeks passed. By August it was almost ready to move into. His father in law, Marshal Jameson, came out on a horse one day and was astounded that all this had been done in such a relative short time. He told Randy he wanted to help some if he could. Randy said, "Well sir, there has to be a lot of firewood cut for that fire place."

Aliel Jameson, retired marshal, devoted husband and father and the father in law to this fine lad had just snookered himself. He would have to use that damn cross cut saw after all. He and Randy laughed at that.

Bill and Aliel went to a patch of dead trees and commenced to saw them down, trim them up and cut them into burnable lengths. After working all day with each other they become friends and spent hours just talking about things in general. By the end of their fifth day Randy told them if they burned that much wood before going back to the desert to live, they were in for some cold weather. The two older men had cut stacks of wood that was twice the size of the house it had to heat.

CHAPTER 25

Randy went to Delfye and gathered her up in his arms and said. "Honey that's the most wonderful news I have ever heard. When do you think it will be due?"

Delfye laughingly said. "Our baby should take about eight more months' to develop and be born. So that puts it about some day in June."

Randy tried to do everything for Delfye after that, so much so that finally Delfye told him he was going to spoil her for life if he didn't cut it out. He laughed and said. "You're right honey, I'll straighten out OK?"

She hugged him and said with a grin. "Now that's better dear."

She had a lesser problem with Bill. He wanted to help, but only succeeded in getting in the way for the most part. She smiled at him and said. "I'm not disabled Bill, so don't jump up and try to help me around this house."

Chastened, Bill said. "I'm sorry gir, I'll stop."

Their planned trip to Yuma had to be put aside due Delfye's pregnancy. They would have to winter here and in fact Delfye needed to be in town because she had grown too much for one child.

Life settled down to a comfort level then. Bill and Randy went to town each week and brought things to make the lodge more comfortable. There were throw carpets for the roughhewn floor and dressings for the windows and bed clothing and mattresses for the three to sleep on. The door that Robert put together was indeed bullet proof. He built it with spruce that he sawed to four inches thick. Above the door Randy had had a plaque made in Denver that read "The Mulehouse Home".

Towards Christmas, Delfye started to look big and have difficulty keeping food down. Now she needed him because she became weak from lack of nourishment. Randy put her on a horse and took her down to Denver to the hospital.

A huge storm moved in that night and dumped snow on the Mountains and torrential rain at lower altitudes. There was no way the two could get home now. The doctor told Randy that his wife was having twins as far as he could tell and they wanted to keep her in for a few days and see if they could settle her down and get her eating again.

Randy went to his in laws and told them. The two went to their daughter's side immediately. Delfye surprised all of them by beginning to eat and keep it down. The doctor told Randy that probably it was worry about being far from help that had caused his wife to have a nervous stomach. Delfye improved enough that by the third day, she was released from the hospital and allowed to go home. Aliel and his wife May opened their arms to the two kids and made them feel right at home. Delfye wasn't a hundred percent yet, but she was holding her own.

The month of July found the two still living with Aliel and May. The flooding from the rain had creeks flooded and rivers impossible to cross. Randy worried about old Bill out by himself. There was plenty of food, wood and things to keep a man for weeks, but still he and Delfye worried. She began to spot blood in late July, so Randy took her to the hospital and they took her right in. The babies were about to be born.

Delfye has a small framed woman and the doctor was worried whether she could deliver a set of twins. He didn't voice his concerns to anyone else. Randy was concerned as well. His wife was having a hard time and he wanted them to help her. Her screams were like daggers in Randy's heart.

The doctor decided to trade two lives for one at some point. He did a C section and it was his first ever. He pulled twin babies from the mother's womb and closed her up. The mortality death rate for this type of operation was almost ninety percent. The twins, one a boy and one a girl would be fine. Time would tell with the mother.

Randy reached for the bottle in his saddle bag and took a long pull on it. He was pretty drunk and his horse Sniffer knew it and walked along slowly. The two were somewhere near the Idaho and California border. There wasn't much to see here in the high desert and Randy was far too drunk to see anything anyhow. He had been drunk for three months now and as far as he could see he might stay drunk for another three.

He would never get over his beautiful wife Delfye dying because of something he did, even if she had helped do it. He began drinking the night he held her in his arms as she took her last breath. He had to be dammed. Every person he touched died or some damn thing. Well he supposed not everyone. His daughter and son lives with his dead wife's mother and father. Old bill had survived the winter and tried his best to console Randy, but alcohol had become his consolation. He never looked at the twin babies before they took them away. He was frozen in fear at what he knew was almost a death sentence for his wife and when she died the following day he left the hospital, went to the bank and drew all the money from the ranch sale out and keeping only enough for his whisky and maybe some food now and then, took it all to Aliel and May and gave it to them then said, "Raise my twins up please, there is more if you need it."

The two were heart broken and just dumbly nodded their heads. They knew Randy wouldn't shake this one so easy and could be on a wild drunk for years now.

Randy hardly remembered the trip across some major mountain and some big valleys. When he got so hungry he had the shakes he killed something to eat. He had flour, bacon and beans in his saddle bags along with two bottles of whisky. Hell he was set for weeks. Randy had the intentions of going over into California and on to the gold fields; although he had no idea as to why. He had more money in a bank account in Yuma Arizona then he could count and he would swap it for one hour with his wonderful wife Delfye.

Sniffer finally stopped in her tracks and Randy leered through his alcohol haze at a rider coming his way. The man stopped a hundred feet from him and waited. Randy wasn't up to company and just sat there and watched the man. Finally the rider inched forward. Randy saw that what he had mistaken for a man was in fact a woman. Randy waited until she was ten feet away before speaking to her. He said. "How do miss?"

The lady cleared her throat and whispered, "Do you have any water Mister?"

Randy said. "Well hell yes I do."

He then held his canteen out to her. She drank deeply and handed it back. Randy said, "Give the horse some girl."

She got down as if she was weak and took her hat off showing pretty brown hair. She poured some water in her hat and let her pony drink it. She took another swallow and handed it back and said more clearly, "Thanks Mister, I hope you know there isn't any water the way you're going. I was almost certain me and my horse was going to die in this desert. I sure was happy to see another human on the trail Mister."

Randy took a long look at the girl. He saw a skinny little sprout of a girl not more than fourteen or fifteen years old. She wasn't a beauty but had an open frank honest looking face and freckles on her nose. He asked her what in the world she was doing way the heck out here in the middle of the desert? She was silent for a minute and then begun a tale that made the hairs rise up on his back and caused him to get madder than hell.

"I'm sixteen and I escaped from my father out in the northern California gold fields. My mother was killed in a rock slide coming north to look for gold. The trail wound around a mountain and when my father and I came around a bend there was a hundred foot piece of the trail missing along with my mother and the horse she road. We could see pieces of her and the horse in the rocks down at the bottom. I was so stunned I almost rode off into nothing. My pony was smart enough to stop or I would have."

Randy stopped her at this point and asked her name. She looked him in the eyes and said. "I'm Jessica Wilkin but most folks call me Jassy."

She continued her story. "My father took my mother's death hard and started to drink a lot. He really scared me a few times, when he got loaded and called me by my mother's name. I could have handled him, except he met this old miner that had struck it rich and insisted I let him openly court me. That wasn't too bad, but what sent me away was when he told the miner he would make a cash deal for me to be the man's wife. I almost got the shot gun down and killed my own father. Instead I lit out on my own. Two men tried to molest me near the California border and I lost all my gear over the deal."

The girl was crying softly and made Randy badly want a drink of whisky, but for some reason he didn't take one.

Randy set and absorbed the strange tale before saying. "You are in a fine pickle girl. You don't even have a bed roll and we are five miles from water. I suggest we head for the river and maybe stick to that."

As they rode along, Randy told her his story and was crying unashamedly as he told it. The girl didn't know what to say, but she felt his pain. She had lost her mother not long ago and the pain was still there, all the time.

The river was more a stream then a river but the water was sweet and cold. It flowed east and that meant they needed to follow it up stream and find some cooler place to camp. Randy couldn't believe he had been drunk for three months and wandered all over the map.

The dry desert had sobered him up and now he didn't need a drink like before. He had run into someone that had worse things to happen to her than what had happened to him {At least he thought so anyhow} Randy kept a lookout for a secure place to establish their camp. When he found one, the girl was hesitant to go in the closed area with him. Randy said, "Look Jassy, please don't think that I'm like other men. You are a child to me and I will look after you, if I'm capable of it."

Jassy made a decision that she had to trust someone and it might as well be this cowboy. She did notice he hadn't taken a pull on his bottle since meeting her. She smiled and said, "If you hurt me Mister I will come back and haunt you for the rest of your life."

Randy laughed then for the first time in three months. He took the bottles and dumped the whisky out on the ground and filled them back up with water from the river then took his pigging string from his saddle and made a strap for them and told the girl they were a poor substitute for a canteen, but better than nothing.

The horse Jassy was riding was so poor that she looked like a mule. The horse was around fifteen years old and probably needed worming because it ate like a, well a horse and was still skinny. He kept a plug of Day's Work chewing tobacco around to worm Sniffer when she got worms. He told the girl to chew some up and don't swallow the juice but make her horse swallow the mess and it would for sure worm her. Jassy surprised him by doing a good job of it. The next time the horse had a bowel movement; Jassy got all excited and exclaimed that it worked by damn. The mess had white moving worms in it. Sniffer stayed as far away as possible from the awful mess. The horse would fatten up some now Randy reckoned.

The girl helped build a fire and with river water boiling, sorted beans and put them in the pot. Randy threw what bacon he had left in with the beans and dumped some salt in for seasoning. Two hours later Randy watched as Jassy tore into the mixture and ate at least half before sitting back and saying. "Mister Thank you for saving this girls life. Those were the best beans I ever ate."

Randy replied with. "I think I must agree with you."

Randy took one of his blankets from his bed roll and gave it to her. He said, "I wish I could do more for you young friend, but I can't."

Jassy began to cry once more and buried her head in her arms. Randy walked away and had his moment of sadness. They were two sad people that fate had thrown together and while Randy didn't much care for company; he couldn't just leave this young girl out in the wilderness alone.

CHAPTER 26

It was freezing and Randy and his charge, "Jassy" were freezing their butts off. The two had ridden south along the bitter root range into what was to become Utah later in the century. The altitude made the air thin and cold. It was September and the north wind had begun to blow last night and it was cold breaking camp early this morning. The girl had Randy's entire bed roll wrapped around her while Randy had on most all his clothes plus his coat. He knew they needed to lose this mountain before the weather would moderate and warm their bones up.

They rode hard all that day and then dropped into a valley where the wind abated and he could build a roaring fire to warm them. Randy hoped it wouldn't snow before the big salt lake came up. It would warm some down there, he hoped.

They topped over a ridge and there was the Great Salt Lake as far as a man could see. Randy reckoned with this much salt in this country the price would never raise much on the stuff. They had ridden hard all day the day before encountering no snow. The weather warmed fast as they descended to the valley floor. The heavy coat and blankets came off as the sun warmed them.

Jassy and Randy had become friends and talked for hours about everything. Randy had kept from her that he was in fact a wealthy man. Once in warmer country Randy began to tell her the whole story. Piece by piece he let it go and when he got to the talking about his ranch Jassy become excited. She exclaimed, "You own a million acre horse ranch in Arizona Territory?"

Randy smiled at her and replied with, "It really didn't seem important until right now girl." Jassy grinned at him and said, "I'm sure glad it means something to you now Randy."

Randy and Jassy rode slowly south along the Colorado River. There were Indians everywhere but they didn't bother the Indians and the Indians didn't bother Randy and Jassy. For some reason he couldn't explain, he held back telling Jassy about his twins living with their grandparents up in Denver. The time just didn't seem right yet.

By November it was cooling down and the two made their way to Yuma. At his bank they dismounted and tied their horses under a shade tree. Jassy said. "I really hope you're not going to rob this bank Randy, because if you are, just let me get gone first."

Randy laughed and said. " I think I own part of this bank honey, so you just sit tight while I go in and get a piece of it OK?"

Jassy said. "Wow you're just full of surprises aren't you Mister."

Randy was still chuckling when the teller asked what she could do for him. Randy was told his balance was almost a million dollars now with the interest building up. He drew out ten thousand in twenty dollar bill paper money. When he walked out, Jassy mounted her horse and waited for him. She asked him, well did you get your piece of the bank Mister. He grinned and said. "Yep, now let's find some place to get clean and I will take you for the best feed this burg has to offer."

The Yuma road house and hotel seemed an excellent place to start. Randy approached the desk and said, "Two single rooms please sir."

The clerk looked him up and down before saying. "Do you think you can afford it sir?"

Randy was instantly on his worst behavior and asked him, "Have you ever heard of the Townsend Lazy eight ranch Mister?"

The clerk grew red in the face and admitted he had indeed and "What, if anything, do you have to do with it sir?"

Randy said, "I just happen to own the damn thing and yes we can afford it, and in fact give me the best suite in this dump of a place."

Jassy had never seen this side of Randy before and grinned from ear to ear at the now red faced clerk. The clerk pulled two keys from boxes behind the counter and handed them over. He went before them saying, "Right this way sir".

Randy thought this was more like it. The rooms were adjoining and as nice as he ever had. The clerk said. "I'll have two hot baths drawn in the bath house at the end of the hall sir."

Randy thanked him and threw his saddle bags on the bed and flopped down beside them. He declared this will do.

Jessica had never seen anything this elegant before and wandered around looking at everything. Randy looked at Jessica's dress and marveled he had never taken notice before. The girl was wearing a tow-sack dress, that a neck and too armholes had been cut in. The dress was bunched at her waist by a short length of small rope. He grabbed her hand and dragged her out of the hotel to a store nearby and told the lady clerk to outfit this young person with at least three of everything and spare no expense. He said. "I'll leave her in your capable hands and ask you to point me to the livery so I can attend to our horses."

The lady pointed down the street on the right. Randy led the horses down and around back to the stable. A hostler was there and Randy paid him to bag feed the two horses and rub them down. He asked where he might buy a buggy and the man pointed across the street at the blacksmiths shop. There wasn't much of a selection of buggy's, just two; one new and one used one. He talked with the owner and some money exchanged hands. He went back to the livery and bought harness and two good horses. Within an hour the buggy was hitched and Randy drove it down to the dry goods store. He went inside to find Jassy sitting beside a mountain of packages with a frightened look on her face. She jumped up and hugged him, saying that she wondered what the heck she would do if he never came back. Randy laughed and paid the bill and he and Jassy carried the packages out to the buggy, which stopped Jassy in her tracks. She said, "Just how much of that bank did you say you owned Mister?"

Randy laughed along with the girl and to his surprise he realized it felt good.

CHAPTER 27

The track to the ranch had been recently traveled and brought back both sad and good memories. The house hove in sight causing a clutching in his heart and wonderment in the young girls heart. They were welcomed by the Mexican care taker and given cool water from the well house to drink.

The place hadn't changed all that much and Jesus {Hey Sus} had gathered all the stray stock into the fields and there were more than Randy reckoned on. There were three hundred head of horses and thirty cows in the bunch. They should have been taken to market last spring but there was no one here to do the job then. Randy and Jesus opened the house and aired it out. Jassy wondered from room to room taking it all in. She didn't want to get too excited yet because this man was a bit of a mystery at times and could put her out on her ear someday, although she doubted it because they had been through a lot together.

"I want you to consider this your home Jassy, for as long as you want, you were dealt a poor hand in life and I have the means to look after you."

There were tears in her eyes as she said. "But who will look after you Randy? You've been hurt worse than I have."

Randy said gently. "You just worry about number one and that's you. If I can help in any way, just let me know."

Jassy went to him and hugged him saying. "I'm sure lucky I ran in to you that day in the desert Mister."

Randy responded with. "No girl. I was on a wild streak and I am the lucky one, you saved me from self-destruction. I haven't had a drop to drink in the four months since I met you. Just make yourself at home and help out anytime you want to."

Jassy fell to the ranch work like her life depended on it. Randy couldn't believe this was the same wayward girl he had met out on the desert near death from starvation and lack of water. She was up at dawn and in the saddle within thirty minutes and seemed to know what needed doing around the ranch. She became a favorite to the brood mares and colts and they ran to meet her each time she rode to their pasture. Jesus the hired man and his family became important to the operation as well. Jesus was a real Mexican cowboy and his wife was one of the best cooks around. Her name was Connie and she flat took over the kitchen and house in general. The herd was multiplying faster than Randy thought it would because every mare was about to drop a foal. The brood mares had gone right on breeding while Randy's world had come apart.

Randy woke up one morning feeling strange and couldn't figure out why until riders came down the trail from the south. There were two of them and they both looked familiar to him. He let go a yell when he recognized old Bill and he had Aliel his father in law with him. They both dismounted and hugged Randy. Bill said. "Boy we have been worried sick about you. The last we heard you were giving it your best shot trying to drink all the whisky in Montana up."

Aliel added. "We rode up there and looked for you, but only found where you had been and had reports that you simply stayed drunk all the time."

Randy said with a pleading look. "I sure want to apologize to the both of you, but for three months last summer I was lost in the bottom of a bottle and didn't have any idea anyone was looking for me. I was fortunate enough to become acquainted with a very young person who needed a helping hand and this person saved me from destroying myself. I haven't had a drink in near six months now."

Bill and Aliel both asked at once, who is this young person? Randy turned to Jassy and said. "This is her, meet Jessica Wilkin, Jassy this is my father in law Aliel Jamison and Bill Townsend who is my uncle. They have been looking for me and I think they knew I'd wind up here eventually."

Jassy shook hands with the two and then excused herself explaining she had work to do down at the corrals, she leaped on a horse and rode out. Bill said. "That gal can handle a horse son, what is your relationship to her now."

The two older men held their breath until Randy said. "Good friends and I am a father figure to her."

Both older men expelled their breaths and laughed together with Randy. Randy went on and told them Jessica's story. They felt their hearts warm towards the girl. Bill said. "She seems contented here on the ranch and is most definitely an asset."

Aliel said. "You have two very beautiful children up in Denver son. I know you had a rough go, but my misses and I are too old to raise two kids that are rambunctious. Do you think you will be able to handle them pretty soon?"

Randy was silent for a time before answering. Finally he asked Aliel if his wife could make it with them until spring time. Aliel said. "I'm sure she will find it hard to let them go at all, but we are old and must do the right thing by the children."

Randy said. "I'll enlist the help of Jassy and we will come to the lodge for the summer and take the two children with us. We will have to spend time getting to know them before we do that too." Aliel Thought this boy is made of the right stuff and I'm proud to know him.

CHAPTER 28

Jessica came to Randy that evening and said. "We need to talk Mister."

Randy said. "So talk young person."

Jassy set down in a chair across from him. She looked him in the eye and said. "You didn't tell me everything did you mister."

Randy smiled and responded with. "If I had, you would have run like a jack rabbit wouldn't you."

Jassy smiled back and said. "You damn betche I would have Mister."

She had a smile on her face however as she said it. Randy asked, "Do you think you want to get to know my two kids?"

Jassy said with a laugh. "You just try and stop me mister."

The winter was a cold one down in the desert this year and the brood mares had to be put in the barn to birth their foals. They found two dead foal that simple froze to death after being in temperatures that reached far below freezing at night. Randy, Jassy and Jesus were kept busy keeping the colts from freezing all the month of February and into the first week of March. The cold spell broke then and things got back to normal.

Randy rode to Yuma and made his deal for the sale of his horses to the army quartermaster at Fort Yuma. There was still a huge demand for horses due the war that was brewing back east and the price was above twenty dollars a head for unbroken gilded yearlings. The demand was so great that the quartermaster agreed to send soldiers to drive the animals from the ranch. Some had to go to Fort Tucson and some had to go to Fort Apache. Randy thought that was fine and simply took the army draft over to the bank and deposited it. He withdrew twenty thousand dollars for their summer in the Rockies and still left a balance of more than a million dollars in his account.

His father in law had ridden back home before the big snows, but old Bill said he couldn't make that trip anymore and needed to thaw his old bones out with some of that hot summer heat. The house would be his for the summer while Randy and Jassy rode horses to Denver.

The summer began early and the heat was suffocating by the time the two reached Gila bend. Randy told Jassy they would ride at night until they reached cooler weather. The horse Randy chose for Jassy was a fifteen hand sorrel that could come close to matching Sniffer for endurance. Their temperament differed however. Sniffer loved her master and the sorrel tolerated hers. She would buck each morning when mounted and according to Jassy it was just for the pure hell of it. Sniffer watched this antic and snorted. The first time it happened Jassy wasn't ready for it and found herself in a mesquite bush butt first. Randy helped her out and watched as Jassy walked around to the front of the sorrel and looked her in the eye. She remounted and spurred the horse until there was no buck left in her. The following morning when Jassy stepped in the stirrup the sorrel took one hop and stopped, rolling her eyes back at her rider. The same ceremony took place each day when first saddled. Her name became old Biddy. Sniffer turned her back on old Biddy anytime Biddy tried to be friendly. The two riders had to laugh at the horses.

CHAPTER 29

Denver was cool compared to the ranch and made them appreciate being there. Randy dropped Jassy it a hotel and gave her some money telling her she could shop for whatever she needed.

He went to the Jameson's to meet his two children for the first time. He rode down the lane and saw two toddlers about the right age playing in a grassed fenced in yard. The two youngsters' came to the fence. Their interest piped by him and Sniffer. The little girl and boy were identical twins, but looked like their mother and put a great sadness in his heart.

His mother in law, May, appeared at the door and smiled at him. He dismounted and tied Sniffer to the hitching post beside the front gate. The gate squeaked as he opened it and entered the yard. His two kids ran to their grandmother and hid behind her skirt, peeping around at him. He smiled and said, "Hello Mrs. Jameson."

She rushed to him and wrapped him in a hug that almost strangled him. His son and daughter clung to her skirt and was drug along with their grandmother. The two kids become frightened and began crying.

Mrs. Jameson bent down and picked them both up. They tried to hide, but had nowhere to go. Mrs. Jameson said. "Now children this is your father and you must look at him."

The boy was the first to move his eyes to his father, then the girl followed suit. Both twins had been coached by the grandparents; that someday their father would come for them. Randy didn't know what to do, but the little girl took that out of his hands by extending her arms out to him and would have fallen to the ground, if Randy hadn't caught her. The boy followed suit after his sister. His heart swelled with the knowledge that his wife had come back to him in these two precious little bundles he held in his arms. Randy croaked out. "What are their names Mrs. Jameson?"

Mrs. Jameson said. "This little girl is named Seceil Delfye Mulehouse and this little boy is named Seth Earl Mulehouse and both have birth certificates to prove it too."

Randy couldn't have put the twins down then if his life depended on it. He said. "Maybe we should go in and sit down."

His legs were weak and they trembled. Mrs. Jameson led them into her house. Randy sat on a chair and looked at his two children and thought, I think my wild days must come to an end.

With responsibilities like these two young persons, he had better settle down somewhere. Then he realized he had been thrown into that wild streak due to events he had no control over. He had lost two wives from them dying on him and another that was unfaithful to him and for the most part couldn't help going a bit wild after each event. Now he had two, No. three young folks; that were dependent on him for their every need in life. He still considered Jassy a child even though he had noticed that she had filled out into a beautiful woman of seventeen. She seemed not to be interested in any boys her age and this worried him some.

The twins hung on to Randy and would cry if someone tried to take them. Mrs. Jameson attempted to take them for their midday feed and was rewarded with wails of anguish from the two. Randy made a decision. The twins would go where ever he and Jassy went effective now by golly. He told Mrs. Jameson his decision and she became teary and hung her head. Aliel caught Randy's eye and nodded his head in approval. Randy said. "We will come back later and get their stuff."

He took off for his horse with two bouncing twins laughing at the way he carried them, he had one under each arm like one would carry a log. The twins loved it and when they reached Sniffer the afore mentioned rolled her eyes at Randy and stood stock still, trembling as Randy stepped in her saddle with the twins, both under his right arm. Once in the saddle, Randy perched one twin in front and the other in the rear and told them to hang on.

He walked Sniffer and he had never seen Sniffer walk so gentle in her life. On the mile and half trip to town the twins bonded with their father and him with them. The one in the rear felt left out and crawled with his help around and sat on Sniffer's neck. Sniffer just snorted and stepped easy.

At the hotel Jassy was waiting on the front porch and when she saw the three coming, tears sprang to her eyes. She rushed to their side and took one of the twins from his hands and set it down on the porch, then took the other one. Both twins were suddenly shy of this girl, but came readily to her without hesitation. They went inside and Randy rented the best rooms the hotel had available. The penthouse on the top floor that sported a kitchen and bath, two bedrooms and a living room. The twins explored the place like prowling cats. They were curious about everything. Jassy was absolutely fascinated and captivated by the two and went where ever they went. She had never been close to any young children in her life and would have to learn as she went. Before the first night passed, the twins had adopted her as their own and would run to her and ask her in rudimentary English about things. Randy had a good feeling each time this happened. Potty training was a sometime funny smelly thing.

Randy had gone out to visit with the Jameson's and to pick up their stuff. When the potty had been loaded on Sniffer she didn't much like the smell of the thing and Randy had to hang on to her to keep her from taking off. He took the potty in and asked Mrs. Jameson to clean it out so his horse would allow it aboard. Aliel got so tickled that he set down on the porch holding his sides. Mrs. Jameson's face turned cherry red, but she scrubbed the pot until when Randy held it up to Sniffer she sniffed it and declared it fit to be on her. When Randy told Jassy about it later, he thought the girl was going to have a seizure from laughing so hard.

The twins were already potty trained, so the messiness came to a halt. Diapers were disposed of with some ceremony. Randy took the whole mess clean and dirty alike and put them in the garbage bin at the rear of the hotel.

He heard shouts and clapping above his head. Looking up he saw his two children and Jassy standing at the window giving those diapers a proper send off.

Randy, Jassy, Seceil and her brother Seth left Denver on four horses. Two were pack horses and they were loaded as high as possible with goods to set up housekeeping out at the Mulehouse lodge. Jassy had never seen the lodge, so Randy had been telling her about it, however nothing Randy had told her prepared her for the impact the falls and his lodge had on her.

When the falls and lodge came in sight they took her breath away and for some reason she didn't understand it caused tears to flow down her face. Randy sensed what Jassy was going through and let her have her little moment without interference. She finally exclaimed. "This is the most beautiful sight this girl has ever seen Mister, let me tell you."

The twins were quiet as a mouse and all eyes. Seth was riding with Jassy and saw the tears and stood on the pommel of her saddle and hugged her neck mouthing what consoling words he knew. Randy thought, "boy, I'm sure glad to be here."

CHAPTER 30

Aliel Jameson stopped his horse and gazed at the setting provided by a wonderful water fall, lodge and surrounding hills. He hated to be one to bear bad news to such a beautiful setting, but his was not the reason or wonder why so he rode on in. Randy saw Aliel and stuck the axe he was splitting wood with in the splitting block. He met Aliel out at the gate and said, "Hello there grandfather to my kids, what brings you up this way?"

Aliel dismounted before he answered Randy. He finally said. "I've got some bad news for you boy, I received a telegram from your caretaker Jesus down on the ranch, you're uncle Bill died a week ago down in Yuma."

He added. "Bill had gone there to see the doctor and keeled over dead right in his office. The doctor stated he was dead on the way to the floor."

Randy was saddened; but knew that Bill had lived a full life and was in a better place in all probability. He and Aliel went in and broke the news to Jassy. The two had been close friends and Jassy cried her heart out.

Randy invited Aliel to spend a while with them and visit with the twins. Aliel was amazed at the growth of the kids. The boy Seth was almost a head taller than his sister Cecile. Both were bright and becoming articulate in the English language. He noticed the two were constant companions to Jassy and the three had their own way of communicating with each other. Few words were spoken except in the presence of Randy. The three simply loved each other. The twins called her Sissy and the name stuck.

Jessica had a problem she couldn't talk to anyone about. She was deeply in love with Randy Earl Mulehouse and he only saw her as a child. It had started way back when Randy had put his bed roll around her to keep her from freezing up in bitter root country, while almost freezing himself to death with only a light coat on. She had tried not to let it happen, but when he had welcomed her to his ranch and they had gone to Denver for the kids and he gave her a bunch of money to buy anything she wanted, all she had wanted to do was to buy Randy something. She resisted the desire, but cried herself to sleep over it.

The whole thing started innocently enough. Randy had gone down to get water at the falls pool and found Jassy taking her bath in the buff. He quickly turned away, but not before seeing one of the most exquisite female bodies he had ever witnessed. He knew his face was red and his heart was fluttering and attempting to jump from his chest. He realized then that Jassy had become a beautiful woman and he had taken no notice of her all this time.

He took the water home and went out and saddled up Sniffer. He threw his bed roll and saddle bags on and rode off. He had to think clearly about this turn of events in his life. Three days later he came home and found a weeping Jassy. The twins were acting concerned as well. Randy went to Jassy and said. "We must talk please."

Jassy stood and followed him outside. He turned and she fell into his arms and all was lost. He asked her,"Will you marry me and be my wife?"

Jassy thought her heart would explode any second. She answered. "Yes, Yes I will."

The twins were peeking out the half open door at them. They looked at each other and just went back to what they were doing. As far as they were concerned the two were already together anyhow, so a little more closeness wouldn't matter a fizz.

CHAPTER 31
15 YEARS LATER

Seth was slightly perturbed at his beautiful twin sister Cecial. She was making eyes at a cowboy and embarrassing the hell out of him. The two were in Denver for the fall Colorado State Fair. The year was 1876 and they were eighteen years old. Seth just couldn't understand why his sister was acting so strange. He liked girls, but he came here with his sister and he meant to stay with her no matter what. The cowboy was a handsome specimen he supposed, but a bit old for his twin. This didn't mean anything to the suitor. He forged ahead and was in the process of seducing his sister and by damn there was gonna be a knock down drag out in a minute. Seth stepped between the man and his sister. He was a good sized boy and stood three inches above the six foot would be seducer. He said, "Go and find someone your own age Mister or suffer the consequence."

He had never been in a fist fight before and was much relieved when the older man backed away and apologized. His sister was livid at him and said. "Brother please don't ever do that again, I can manage my own affairs thank you, very much."

She stomped off in a huff in the opposite direction than Romeo took. It only took three minutes before another boy had his tongue hanging out for his twin sister. Seth threw his hands up and took off. Maybe she could handle herself. He walked until he saw his Dad and Jassy at one of the food stands. They both smiled at him. Jassy asked, "Where is your sister son?"

Seth said. "Being chased by every male at the fair, that's where."

Randy laughed and said, "Well find you a female you can chase son."

Seth was shocked to hear his father talk like that and his face turned red. Jassy said. "Honey don't embarrass our boy that way."

She had a twinkle in her eye however and the parents locked eyes and then laughed. Seth said. "Aw, I don't see any that interest me Sassy and if I did I wouldn't take up with her, because I came here to be with my family and not some stranger."

His seriousness sobered the two parents up from their laughter. They realized their son was mature beyond his eighteen years and went about the rest of the day with him.

The three ran into Cecial and she was still alone and had gotten over her mad spell and laughed and joked with Seth. She said. "Brother you must have scared that man half to death. I ran into him and he took off like he was bee stung and there was a woman that had been walking with him and she looked totally confused."

Randy said, "In all probability that confused woman was that man's wife."

Seth exclaimed, "I should have pounced his butt and now I'm sorry I didn't." The entire family cracked up with laughter then.

Seth had an idea that maybe he wanted to explore the Rocky Mountains west of the lodge and approached his Dad about it. His father thought that would be a wonderful thing for him to do and set about helping him get his gear together. Randy threw a saddle on a bronco and remembered old Sniffer, and was sad for a minute. Sniffer had reached the ripe old age of twenty-three before Randy stopped riding her.

She was put to pasture in the little valley behind the lodge and one morning two summers ago Randy found her dead. He cried like a baby.

He had never set a better horse than Sniffer. He couldn't become attached to another after she passed. For one thing she was irreplaceable and for another if he found another Sniffer, it had to compare to her because he would have to go through loosing that one too.

Seth was all ready to go and mounted up when Cecial came at a run with tears streaming down her face. She grabbed her brother's leg and said. "You can't leave me behind brother; I want to see the Rocky Mountains too."

Randy threw up his hands and went to catch up another horse. He supposed these two would be together their whole life. Randy had heard of such case's, but never dreamed his twins would be that close.

CHAPTER 32

Seth woke up with fear coursing through every part of his body. He looked over where his sister was supposed to be sleeping and knew why. She wasn't there and even her sleeping roll was gone. He heard her scream then and followed her voice and saw she was being drug from camp bed roll and all.

Her attacker was a Grizzle Bear of such huge proportions that Seth's heart almost stopped. He didn't try to dress before he grabbed his Henry Rifle and in his stocking feet and long johns ran for his sisters life. The bear was going slower than normal because of the sleeping gear kept tripping him up. Seth drew a bead on a spot just behind the bear's right ear and pulled the round off. The Henry bucked and the bear stood straight up to its full height and fell over backwards flinging his sister through the air for ten feet or so. Cecial landed limply and didn't move. Seth ran to her and saw that her face and shoulder had deep lacerations in them, but she was breathing. He reached under her and picked her up keeping his gun in his hand. He went to the camp fire and quickly found some clean clothing to tear into bandages. He took alcohol and cleansed her wounds and bound them up. She had bled some from the head wound but seemed to be breathing quietly.

Seth dressed and then saddled two horses. He took his sister in his arms and mounted one of the horses. He left camp at a lope leading the other horse. He had cut their two pack horses loose and they ran right along with them. Seth figured they weren't more than five miles from the lodge. It was very early on their third day of exploring the Rockies and hadn't gotten far from home.

Randy and Jassy heard the horses coming and knew there was trouble. Randy was out of bed and outside by the time the four horses came to a stop. One look and he knew his beautiful daughter was dead, because there was far too much blood on the saddle for her not to be. Seth shouted. "She's still alive Dad take her please."

Randy took her in to the house and as was the custom in those days laid her on the dining room table. Jassy had stoked up a cook stove and pulled some Luke warm water from the stove well to clean Cecile's wounds. Cecial was still breathing lightly but was unconscious. Seth was beside himself at his failure of keeping his sister safe and was beating up on himself pretty bad.

Randy told him he should maybe not be so hard on himself because these things happen in life. They worked on Cecial for an hour and she finally came around and had a bad moment remembering the bear dragging her away. When Seth told her that he had killed the bear with one shot behind the ear, she said. "Thank you brother for saving my life."

Seth got red in the face and looked down at his boots. Randy told Seth he should ride to Denver and see if Doc Mundry felt like coming out to stitch Cecial's wounds up. Seth took a fresh horse and rode like fire to Denver and brought young Doctor Stanly James Mundry into Cecial's life and changed it forever.

The ride out to the Mulehouse lodge was something new to Doctor Mundry. He had often thought of riding out here because his heart throb lived there. He had met Cecial at the fair when she was nineteen years old and thought she had to be the most beautiful girl in the entire wild west. He being the chief surgeon at Denver proverbs hospital kept him very busy and there wasn't much time left in his eighteen hour day to chase girls. His heart had beat a little faster when Seth Mulehouse had ridden in and ask if he minded making a house call. When Seth explained what had happened his actions had become more hurried. The chance of infection increased the longer the wounds were left unattended to.

The Doctor was a born Denverite and kept a horse at the livery. He asked Seth if he would go and saddle his mount while he put together a mini surgical package in a large bag. By the time Seth returned with his horse, the young doctor was pacing outside the hospital and when they were mounted he rode like Cecial's life depended on it and in fact did. If infection set in, in one of the deep lacerations near her head she would die. A limb can be removed to rid a body of infection, but not a head.

The doctor took one look at Cecial and it almost broke his heart. This young girl would be disfigured for life unless he did some miracle work. Her head was laid open in a six inch long gash that would require a hundred stitches at least. He had trained in Boston and a new concept of scar less stitching had been shown to the medical students. Stanly had never had an opportunity to put it in practice however, until now. He administered Laudanum to deaden Cecial's pain and operated on each laceration in turn and made sure any suspected infection causing flesh was removed. This was a long drawn out process he couldn't hurry up and he had to keep the Laudanum flowing. Cecial followed him with her eyes and knew he was good and just maybe she would survive this bear attack after all.

The operation and subsequent stitching took seven hours of mind numbing work to complete. Stanly was completely exhausted when Cecial went peacefully asleep. Randy had Jassy to prepare some food for the doctor. They sat on the front porch to eat. The doctor had to say something, so he got right to it. He said. "We can only pray that no infection sets in now and if it does I must cut it out immediately, so you have me as a house guest until your daughter and sister is out of danger."

Day turned into night and every time Cecial woke up the good doctor was there by the bedside where she had been moved to. One time he wasn't and she cried out for him and he came running. She said. "Oh I thought you had gone away from me."

His heart thumped in his chest and he replied that he would never go away from her again. Cecial attempted to smile but it hurt, so she went back to sleep.

The large tear on her face would heal up, but some of the small abrasions were becoming weepy; a prelude to infection. Doctor Mundry operated on each one and removed the infected flesh from the wound. He was sure her system would take over soon and he was right. On the fourth day she sat up in bed and said through her bandages that she was hungry. The relief her family felt was a joyous thing to behold. Doctor Stanly James Mundry was visible shaken and moved to happy tears, both Randy and Jassy took note of. The young doctor loved their daughter and from the looks that the two exchanged she was in love with him as well.

The wedding was the most talked about event in Denver that fall. Young Doctor Mundry was going to marry the scared but still beautiful daughter of Randy and Jessica Mulehouse. They would live in Denver where he had built a brand new house for that purpose. What the doctor didn't count on was that, the deal included both Mulehouse twins. Seth did leave his sister alone with the doctor so that the two consummated their marriage, but as soon as the chief surgeon returned to his eighteen hour days at the hospital; Cecial and Seth rode the hills around Denver daily together like the twins they were.

CHAPTER 33

Randy and Jassy had a wonderful relationship and daily talked things out. Jassy said, "I haven't been feeling well of late dear and don't know what, if anything is wrong, but I think I should be looked at by a doctor."

Randy turned cold all over as blood rushed to his head. He had tears in his eyes as he said a silent prayer. He didn't waste time getting her down to their son-in-law doctor.

"You have a blood disease that is aggressive by nature Jassy and the only known treatment is transfusion of new blood into your body which doesn't really help most of the time."

Jassy said. "Well maybe it will work this time son, let's try it."

While Jassy was upbeat, all Randy could think about was he had lost three wives so far and stood to lose his fourth to a blood disease. He was devastated and withdrawn. The blood transfusions were a painful thing for Randy to watch.

He remembered the day he had met this wonderful person out on the hot high desert and the life they had built together and prayed to God the transfusion would work. He needed his wife and couldn't imagine life without her.

The doctor said. "Well Jessica you've beat the odds and I can't find any signs that you have any blood disease what so ever."

Randy felt like the world had been lifted off his shoulders. He went outside the doctor's office and let go a war whoop that was heard all the way down at the front desk.

Randy told Stanley he was the best damn doctor in the world and that was the ever living truth. Stanley was happy for the two, but knew in his heart the cure might not stick. He kept that to himself. Randy told the doctor he wanted to take him and his star patient out for a steak dinner and right now by damn. The doctor decided he was hungry and accepted the invitation with joy in his heart.

They went to the Western Hotel down on Main Streer. They had steak and all the trimmings. Stanley noticed that Jassy only picked at her food. He knew this was a bad omen. His thoughts were, let them have what time together they could. If he had to, he would have another blood drive and re do the transfusion.

CHAPTER 34

Randy pulled his horse Sniffer II up and gazed at the water hole. He saw recent tracks down to the spring but no sign of anyone. He moved Sniffer II down the bank of the ravine and on to the water pool. Sniffer II was thirsty and Randy stopped and dismounted short of the spring and led his horse up to the water. Randy took a half empty bottle from the right saddle bag and removed the cap. He upended it and swallowed two ounces of rot gut whisky. It burned to the bottom of his empty stomach and attempted to rise back up. He swallowed fast and held it down.

Randy was in the Bitter root Mountains south of Idaho. He came because, he wanted to find Jessica's father and inform him of his daughter's death. Jassy had gone downhill so fast that it near destroyed him and she was in so much pain near the end, that Randy felt relief that his wife would suffer no more. She was lucid right up to the end and Seth and Cecial had been there when the end came.

Cecial and Seth would live with Stanly while he went on another WildStreak. He had never thought of his father in law one time, until Jassy mentioned that maybe he could find him and tell him she forgave him for everything.

The last known place her father had been was over in California near Mount Shasta, near a place called Weed. There was gold in the foothills of Mount Shasta and John Wilkin had a claim up a ravine somewhere. Jassy had given the best directions she could remember and then she died.

That was three months ago. He had ridden to Newcastle and found that his friends Lasiter and Jody Holt had moved to a ranch and been massacred by a marauding band of Sioux Indians back five years before. That was when Randy said the hell with it and bought a bottle of whisky. He had lost some of the best friends he had and needed to forget someway and a ninety cent bottle of whisky was a cheap escape from reality.

Randy had for the last three months wandered through out the high plains of Wyoming and Montana. He ran into a few Indians from time to time, but there was a mystery about him that warded strangers both

Indian and white away from him. He would long for his children, but then he still had to go.

His son Seth told his father that he would stay behind and take care of the Lodge and his twin sister. Randy thought he should turn back now, but he had to honor his dying wife's wish and he would or die trying.

CHAPTER 35

Randy rode into Weed, California on a cold rainy evening and sought some place to dry out. There was a livery and he started there. His mouse colored gray had had a tough time in the mountains east of here and could use a good feed of oats. He rode in the yard and was met by the hostler. The man was abrupt but friendly.

"Whatche need Mister?"

Randy said, "Some feed for this worn out horse and some information if you don't mind."

The hostler didn't say anymore, he went to a feed bag and filled a nose bag with oats and handed it to Randy. Sniffer lit into the oats and munched away. Randy asked if there was a hotel in the town and the hostler nodded his head yes and said, "Across the street and down a bit,"

He hesitated then said, "You look like a pretty good sort sir and this town is crammed full of some of the most dishonest men in this country. If you go in the saloon and you must if you want to eat, someone will try to pick you. You would be better off putting that six gun in your saddle bags unless you can use it well."

Randy appraised the man and liked what he saw. He said, "I can use it sir don't worry."

The man was older than Randy by some ten years and said, "My name's Baldy Jones what's yours?"

Randy told him and he asked, From down Denver way? Randy said. "Yes I am, why?"

Baldy had indeed heard of Randy Mulehouse and knew he could use a gun. He replied with. "I was in Dead Wood South Dakota a few years back and now I remember seeing you out draw a bad looser and kill him. We talked about that for years around Dead Wood. No one blamed you and that was the fastest draw any of us had ever seen." He shook Randy's hand saying. "I'm proud to meet you Mister. Give me a little time and I'll make sure the locals understand not to start anything they can't finish."

Randy walked to the saloon and with misgivings aplenty, but went in through the two swinging doors. There was a poker game going on at the rear of a room that resembled a church by its size. A bar that was battered but shiny stood along the left side of the room. There were two men bellied up there drinking. Randy skipped the bar and walked straight to a group of tables that occupied the center of the huge room. He hooked a chair with his toe and sit down. A young girl timidly approached him. She asked, "How can I help you sir?"

Randy said, "I'll have something to eat please and make it whatever is the special of the day."

The girl smiled and disappeared through a door that swung two ways. One of the men at the bar detached himself and walked over. Randy saw it was the hostler Baldy Jones and said. "Howdy Mr. Jones I see you are enjoying a beer."

Baldy replied, "Yeah it's the only thing cold in this town to drink."

Randy was curious and asked Baldy how in the world the bar kept the beer cold. Baldy laughed and replied with. "They cut ice from the mountain lakes in the winter and bring chunks down here and store it in saw dust to keep it from melting and it cools beer the whole summer."

Randy told Baldy he would buy them each a beer if he Baldy would go get them. Baldy was only too happy to do just that, because a hostler didn't make a lot of money and he couldn't afford to drink nickel beer all night.

While Baldy was gone, his food came and someone had gone out of their way to cook a great tasting meal. Randy hadn't had a real meal since leaving home and he did it justice. Baldy kept up a steady stream of interesting conversation while he ate. Randy noticed Baldy paid a lot of attention to what Randy was eating and called the little waitress over and whispered that she should bring his friend the same meal and he would pay for it.

The girl disappeared once more and Randy could hear a muted slinging of pots and pans out in the kitchen that made him smile.

While waiting for Baldy's food, Randy engaged his new friend in conversation about Weed, California. Baldy was a good source of information. Randy wanted to know how he got the name Baldy. Baldy reached one hand up to his hat and lifted it and the answer was clear. Baldy was as bald as a billiard ball. They both got tickled at that. Baldy's food came and he was stunned and grew red in the face while saying, he couldn't pay for this food. Randy held his hands up and said, "On me my friend, I have been fortunate in life as far as money is concerned and you seem like a good man in an unfortunate position, so please take it in the spirit in which it's given."

Baldy placed a level look on him and said. "You are one good man Mr. Mulehouse, Thank you from the bottom of my heart."

Baldy fell on the food like a hungry hound pup. He didn't say one word until his plate was wiped clean with the last bit of roll. He looked up and said. "I'm forever indebted to you Mr. Mulehouse."

Randy said. "Well there is one thing you need to get over pretty quick Baldy and that is my name is Randy and not Mr. anything Ok?"

Baldy grinned from ear to ear and said. "You got it Randy. Now what did you really come to this God forsaken place for anyhow."

Randy was surprised that this man was much more than met the eye. He asked, "Would you consider being an employee of mine on say a hundred a month and found?"

Baldy set back with a shocked look on his face and thought, man that's four times what I make now, not counting the found bit. He answered with an explosive, "Yes. What do we do first and who do we kill?" They both laughed.

CHAPTER 36

Randy and Baldy walked to the livery before Randy said anything. When they were inside, he and Baldy sit down in chairs and Randy told him the story of his dead wife Jessica Wilkin. When Randy finished Baldy said slowly. "There is a John Wilkin that mines a claim out a few miles, but he's not a real friendly sort and has shot at some folks that got too close to his claim. Could this be your dead wife's father?"

Randy nodded his head and replied that the man sounded like the description given him by Jassy the day he found her.

Randy held up his hand and Baldy stopped his horse and the two pack horses in their tracks. Randy dismounted and led Sniffer back to them. He said quietly that this could be the place and they should move a little farther back for safety.

Randy walked Sniffer past the pack animals and remounted. He and Baldy rode until they found a well defendable campsite. They set up camp and cooked a meal. To Randy there was no hurry now and they should move slowly in their attempts to contact John Wilkin.

The voice scared the hell out of Randy and he set up in his bedroll. Baldy did the same and both were looking up a shotgun barrel. Randy said. "Easy friend we mean you no harm,"

The man repeated his words that had scared them both awake. "What are you doing on my claim?"

Randy replied with, "We didn't know this was anyone's claim Mister, and you had better pull that shotgun up or use it, because you just don't throw down on someone that means you no harm."

Randy wasn't really bluffing because he had his forty-four under the covers and it was cocked and aimed more or less at John Wilkins heart. John Wilkin's face went through several changes and he did raise the shotgun some and point it at the now dead campfire.

Randy moved the covers back and exposed the forty-four in his hand. Wilkin jerked and almost made the biggest mistake in his life by bringing the shotgun back around. Randy shook his head causing Wilkin to stop. Fear then clutched the man's heart after he realized he would have been dead if this man had just pulled the trigger on his gun. Randy said gently. "Lay the shotgun aside and join us for breakfast Mr. Wilkin."

John Wilkin realized this man knew who he was and that worried him a great deal. He blurted out. "Where do I know you from stranger?"

Randy got up from his bed roll before answering the man. He told Baldy to put a fire together and make some coffee and biscuits with bacon. He appraised his father in law for a bit and then said, "You don't know me Mr. Wilkin, but I have heard all about you for the last twenty-two years or so. I was making my way across the high desert north and east of here twenty-two years ago when I ran in to a waif of a girl not yet sixteen and I saved her and her horse's life by giving them both some water."

He noticed John Wilkin turning white in the face, but he continued. "This little lost girl saved this drunks life by giving me something and someone to care about in life, because my wonderful wife of two years had died in my arms of childbirth and I turned to a bottle of whisky to console my broken heart. That little girl over the next twenty-two years mended my broken heart and become the step mother to my twin children."

John Wilkin really made a serious mistake then by saying. "What does this have to do with me mister and you still haven't answered why you are on my claim."

Randy lost it then and grabbed him by his shirt front and slammed him into a tree trunk. He put his face right up to the man's face and said, "You piece of cow shit, we're talking about your daughter Jessica. Remember you tried to put her with some dirty old man and she took off and damn near died in the desert?"

John Wilkin was whimpering by the time he wound down enough to drop him like a sack of wheat on the ground. He asked the man if he remembered Jessica at all. Randy had tears streaming down his face by this time and really didn't expect an answer from this revolting man. He continued on by saying, "I am here because I promised Jessica Mulehouse Nee Wilkin I would inform her father that she forgives you. Why I don't know, I wish I had shot your worthless ass when you had a gun trained on me."

Randy walked away with the words. "Get your worthless carcass out of my camp and leave the shotgun, because I wouldn't put it past you to shoot a man in the back simply because you're a coward. I'll leave the gun with the sheriff in town or the saloon keeper; whichever one I see first, now get."

John Wilkin scuttled like a crab out of camp still whimpering. Baldy shook his head and said.

"Damn man, I'm sure glad you and I are friends. I think that man will never be the same again."

Randy apologized to Baldy by saying. "I'm sorry you had to see that Baldy, but I sure needed to get it out of my system."

CHAPTER 37

Seth heard the riders coming long before he saw them and was waiting out front of Mulehouse lodge when they came up. He didn't know the one man, but he recognized his Dad and put his Sharps down on the porch. He went to them and as they dismounted, wrapped his father in a bear hug that squashed the wind out of him. Randy laughed and said. "Boy you don't have any idea how strong you are. How's your Sister and Stanley getting along?"

Seth looked at Baldy and Randy said, "I'm sorry son this is our newest hired hand; my friend Baldy Jones."

Seth shook Baldy's hand and said. "Glad to make your acquaintance sir."

Randy looked at his son and thought; my boy has some good manners about him. Seth said, "Cecelia and Stanly were just up here and I'm surprised you didn't run into them."

Randy explained that he and Baldy came down the mountain trail and never hit Denver.

Seth said, "Well Cecil is having some babies and they wanted to tell me about it."

Randy caught the babies bit and grabbed Seth and shook him and shouted, "Did you say babies?"

Seth laughed and said, "I did dad and I mean triplets and Stanly told me he expected no problems what so ever."

Randy thought my family really is growing now for sure.

CHAPTER 38
THE LAST HURRAH

Randy Mulehouse caught his reflection in the full length mirror on the door of his suite. He thought he still cut a fine figure for a man nearing sixty years of age. He was in Yuma Arizona at the turn of the century. His dress depicted a well to do man, his hat was a white Stetson, his suit was gabardine, colored dove gray and his boots were soft leather western high tops with a walking heel.

He was a man fit and trim with steel gray eyes and salt and pepper hair that he kept trimmed short. All in all he looked the part of a successful rancher and that was exactly what he was.

Randy had left his mountain retreat in Colorado and been living and operating his vast ranch now for two years. He had been so deep in sorrow after Jessica's death, that all he wanted was a place to hide. He and Baldy left the Lodge and rode to the ranch. Baldy had been the one to pull it all together and still was the glue that held it all to gather.

Randy's children Seth and Cecial had visited last Christmas and brought the three grandchildren down too. The triplets named Bonny, Robby and Randy. Were nice kids but too young to really bond with their grandfather. He promised he would visit come spring, and meant to keep his word.

Yuma was a rip roaring border town and the bars and canteens stayed open all night every night.

Randy had come to town to oversee the loading of the eight wind mills he had ordered in. He needed water so he could grow alfalfa and oats on his own land. The cost of hay had doubled over the last two years and it would become unprofitable soon to raise horses that way.

The windmills had been shipped by Wells Fargo freight lines and were due to arrive sometime this week. He had some other business to take care of too and went out of the hotel and over to his bank.

His banker was always glad to see him and escorted him to his private office. Randy told him he needed to make some changes in his account and first needed an update on how it stood.

The banker went out and came back in with a slip of paper in his hand. He laid the paper down in front of Randy. Randy looked at and whistled. He had no idea his money had grown so. He was approaching the two million mark. The horses had really done good.

He said. "I want to open two other accounts in my children's names. Their names are Seth Mulehouse of Denver and his twin sister Cecial Mundry of the same city. I want to put two hundred and fifty thousand in each account. Here are the mailing addresses and they need to be notified."

The banker complied without a word. The money was to remain right here until the twins decided to use it.

Randy decided he needed a cup of coffee. He walked from the bank over to a small restaurant and went inside. The place was warm and comfortable. He sat at a table and a waitress came and took his order for toast and coffee.

He looked out the window and saw the morning stage from Tucson. It was unloading at the stage stop hotel where he was staying. He saw two men exit the carriage and then his heart lurched in his chest. He knew better, but he could swear he saw his long dead wife Salena step from the coach. Randy without realizing it was on his feet and headed for the door. The waitress was left standing with a cup of coffee and a plate of toast.

Randy almost ran to the Stage Stop Hotel. He went straight to the desk and there she was. Randy was coming apart at the seams. He approached the woman and she turned and saw him and smiled the same sweet smile he remembered. He almost fainted. He stuttered out something like, "But you're dead Salena."

The smile disappeared from the woman's face. She asked, "What did you call me Mister?"

Randy could see subtle differences between this woman and Salena now that he was up close. He quickly recovered and apologized for being forward. The lady smiled once more and said, "You have mistaken me for my half-sister Salena Townsend who died some years ago. My name is Virginia Townsend, from North Carolina, and who might you be sir."

Randy was near fainting again. He sat down and asked her to do the same. He couldn't stand up any longer. He finally got his emotions under control and tried to explain. He told her his name and recognition came in her eyes. She said, "Oh my goodness, you're the one I came out here to see Randy."

Her face grew pink and she corrected the name to Mr. Mulehouse sir. Randy held his hand up and said. "You will have to forgive me Virginia, but you just gave me the shock of the century a few moments ago. Do you have any idea how much you resemble my dead wife?"

Virginia grew more pink and said, "My father was her father and that makes me illegitimate. I always knew he was my father, but my mother just suffered in silence even though she was the one to opt out of the relationship. He sent money up until his death, but by that time we really didn't need it anyhow. I'm not here to cause any problems in your life sir, I just want to see my father's grave.

Randy said. "Well let's get you settled and we can talk it out over dinner this evening ok?"

Virginia leveled a look at this handsome man and felt a twinge in her chest. She smiled and shook his hand and agreed. Her hand continued to tingle for a half hour after the hand shake.

Randy rushed back to the coffee shop and apologized to the waitress. The girl was all smiles and simply redid the order. Randy couldn't get his mind off, Virginia, she was some years older than Salena, because she was born before Salena's mother Joanlea married Salena's father. Her age had to be around forty something. He wondered if she was married, he had seen no rings and she seemed more like a single lady, than an old married one.

Randy closed his eyes and tried to picture Salena, but all that come up was Virginia's face. Aw hell he had done it again and he was too damn old for this. There had been no other since Delfye and he had thought he was finished with women for life, now look what he had walked into. He hoped he was wrong, but deep down knew better.

CHAPTER 39

Randy came awake with a start, someone was at his door. He said, "One moment please."

He pulled on a shirt and his trousers and went to the door. It was the Hotel clerk with a telegram from Seth. He grabbed his glasses and read it. "Hello Dad, we thought you might not mind if we came down a bit early. The kids are antsy to see their grandfather. We will go straight to the ranch. We called and Baldy informed us you are in Yuma. We'll see you soon, Seth."

Randy set there and savored the warm feeling he always got from conversing with his son. The house would be full of three rambunctious kids for Christmas. Randy called the desk and placed a call to his ranch. Baldy came on the line and he and his boss had a good talk about how things were going out there. Randy then told him there would be a house full of kids and adults for Christmas. Baldy, who was like family now, was happy. The three kids doted on him, and could have their way with him.

Randy thought it might be a bit premature to reveal the strange meeting with his half-sister in law, Virginia Townsend. He would wait, because none of the other members of his family had ever met his wife Salena that had died out on the trail.

Randy went to the small restaurant for breakfast he had been in the afternoon when Virginia had almost destroyed his world. He had meant to take her to dinner last night, but had gone to the Cattleman's club and drink enough scotch that he wouldn't have been good company anyhow. He hadn't drank in such a long time that it hit him harder than he thought it would. He had been pretty tipsy when he walked to his room last night.

He ordered a full meal, because he hadn't eaten last night. When the food came, he didn't fool around, he simply devoured the eggs, bacon and biscuits. The waitress kept his coffee cup full. After the meal he walked to the hotel and inquired at the desk if Miss Townsend was in the hotel. The clerk got a confused look on his face. He answered with, "I'm sorry sir but there is no Miss Townsend staying here."

Randy's heart turned cold at the clerk's words. Randy said, "She was here with me yesterday afternoon, and I'm sure she was booking into a room."

The clerk went to his register and searched and shook his head. He said. "We only had one new arrival yesterday sir, and that was a Mrs. Virginia Waterman and here she come right now."

Randy turned around and saw Virginia coming down the stairs. She was stunning in a riding habit with a skirt that was made for side saddle riding and a white shirt. Randy met her at the bottom of the steps. She smiled at him and said good morning Mister Mulehouse. Randy cringed at the formal use of Mister and knew he should do something about it, but was stricken by this person that resembled her sister so much.

Randy apologized for not showing up for their impromptu dinner date, he told her he'd had something to come up, and he had to take care of. He left out the part that the something was to have one more last drink with his long dead wife.

Randy said. "Let me take you to breakfast to make up for last night."

Virginia smiled at him and said. "That is a wonderful idea sir."

Randy said. wait a minute, Virginia, "I want you to drop the sir and mister stuff, ok? You are invited to call me Randy, please."

Virginia smiled the same sweet smile her sister Salena did all those years ago, almost causing Randy to cry. She said. "Randy I think that's a grand idea. Now let's go and eat because I am starved to death."

Virginia took his arm and caused Randy to almost swoon. He hoped he could get over comparing her to her sister. He thought he could, in time anyway.

Randy walked her to the Cattleman's restaurant just down the street. The waitress took them to a table in the back and seated them. Randy hadn't been with any other woman in so long, that it felt strange now being here with this beautiful creature,

He began the conversation by asking her about the strange last name. Virginia laughed and it sounded like water trickling over a falls. She said. "My mother lived with a man named Samuel Waterman for most of my life; I assumed the name, because he was a father to me until he died of a heart condition a few months back. My mother died last year and I took care of Sam after she died, because he was nearing ninety years of age."

Virginia wanted to know all about him and Randy filled her in on the important parts anyway. He left out the wild drinking sprees he had gone on after each wife died, he was kinda regretful he hadn't had tough enough moral fiber in him to pull his boot straps up and keep his life on the straight and narrow.

He was silent too long, remembering. Virginia said. "Well, Randy Mulehouse, you have withstood some devastating episodes in your life, but it appears to me you have come through unscathed by all that has happened to you. My half-sister knew what she was doing when she chose you for her husband and I hope to be a friend to you and I want to see this ranch you own too. I would like to say, Samuel Waterman turned over a fortune to me when he passed on and the banks do bulge back in Raleigh North Carolina. So put away any fears that you might have, I'm not here to try and take away from you Randy. I'm here because I have no other place I want or need to be."

CHAPTER 40
THE HOME COMING

Randy set high in the seat of his rubber tired buggy as he came in view of his ranch. Virginia sitting beside him took a deep breath and let it out in a long sigh. She had her hands clasped at her chest and was thrilled to the depth of her soul. She took in all the horses and the beautiful house with the huge barn and at the pure neatness of it all.

Virginia scooted over next to Randy and plastered her body against his. He thrilled and was glad he and her had gotten along so well. She understood his feelings for her long dead sister and never brought it up. Randy had dealt with it the only way he knew, he thanked God for his wisdom of sending this wonderful creature to him. The two had spent a wonderful week in Yuma and Randy would never forget the first time he took her to bed. It had been in his suite. It was totally unplanned by either one of them and Randy had known no passion any sweeter nor intense.

He had been totally satisfied and Virginia had been as loving as her sister after, so Randy had asked her to be his wife and she accepted with another round of passion, that left Randy drained.

The windmills had arrived and should be at the ranch and maybe were being installed. Baldy had been on top of what he wanted from the windmills. They needed a steady stream of water that could be directed at any one of the one million acres that bordered the Gila River on both sides. The vast part of the land was on the south side, but Randy had inspected the north side and found some rich soil there too, where the river had run at some earlier time.

As he and Virginia approached the ranch, they saw three windmills turning and the sight gave Randy a thrill. He had a moment of remembering why he and Salena had gone on that fateful trip that she failed to survive. He hoped Salena was looking down and looking at the windmills pumping water to the elaborate irrigation system he and Baldy had built.

Randy and Virginia didn't even stop at the house; the windmills were like a magnet pulling them to the river. The windmills were being installed above the normal high water mark, inside a levy system that would hopefully protect them from future floods. There was a cement tank that was estimated to hold a half million gallons of water and would double as a snake free swimming hole. Water would be siphoned from this above ground tank and would flow wherever Baldy wanted it to.

Randy and Virginia stopped at the cement pond and debarked from the buggy. Randy saw the water from three windmills flowing into the one quarter full pond and thrilled at the long dreamed reality of it. Baldy was there and shook Randy's hand. He became shy as he noticed Virginia and found the toe of his scuffed boots interesting. Randy said. "Baldy, I would like you to meet my new wife, Virginia."

Baldy really looked at Virginia then and got a scared look in his eyes, He turned white as a sheet and stuttered out that she was Salena. "The picture of you hangs in the living room of the house!"

He was about to come unglued, until Randy said. "Baldy this is the older sister of Salena and don't feel bad about your reaction. It mirror's mine the first time I met her."

Baldy sat down on the buggy's tail end and took his hat off. He wiped his bald pate with a red bandana and swore he felt like he had seen a ghost. Virginia walked over to him and put her hand on his shoulder then asked, "Does that felt like a ghost?"

Baldy stood and told her no it didn't and he, by golly was proud to meet her. Randy smiled at the two.

Randy took Virginia up to the house and inside. The two had no more stepped into the living room when there was a piercing scream from the kitchen and a loud thump, like someone falling down. Randy ran to the kitchen to see Connie their cook laying on the floor all covered with flour and some other sticky stuff. He thought she must be dying. Before he could get to her, her husband Jesus (hey suse) came from out of nowhere and had her in his arms. Just about that time Virginia stuck her head in the room and Jesus, turned his head and screamed much as his wife had. He turned white and began to tremble all over. Randy thought he was going wind up on the floor with Connie any second. He decided he had better divulge who Virginia really was. Both of the two had watched Salena grow up and had suffered a great sorrow when she had died, now here she was in the flesh.

Randy hadn't thought far enough ahead to prevent this. He grabbed Jesus and hustled him out the back door and sat him at a bench in the back court.

Randy shook Jesus by his shoulders until he had his attention. He then said slowly while looking in the man's eyes. "That woman is Salena's sister from back east."

Jesus took two minutes to assimilate that in his brain. The light finally went on and Jesus crumpled on the bench and great tears flowed down his cheeks. He grabbed Randy and said. "I still miss her so and pray for her every night."

Randy couldn't hold back the tears then. The two grown men sat there and bawled like babies.

Virginia and Baldy found them there like that, Jesus suddenly sit up and said, "Connie!" Virginia said quickly that she had put her in one of the bed rooms after a cleanup and she was sleeping peacefully. Jesus bolted for the door and went inside and it was a good thing, because they all heard the scream she let go when she woke up. Randy took off too. He found Jesus firing Spanish at his wife while she made sounds and nodded her head. Baldy and Virginia made an appearance then and Connie and Jesus stopped talking as their eyes grew big and round. Virginia smiled that same sweet smile and both of the Mexicans started bawling again. Virginia rushed over and got down on her knees and said. "I'm not my sister, but I really do need some true friends like you two."

All three of them had a good cry, Baldy and Randy snuck out and went out back. Randy looked at Baldy and said. "I need a drink, how about you friend."

Baldy said. "If you're buying I'm damn sure drinking one."

The two friends went to Randy's private liquor cabinet that hadn't been opened for over two years and Randy pulled out a bottle of the best scotch he had and opened it up, poured three fingers in two water glasses and toasted his friend. He said. "It's been a long trip my bald headed friend, but I think I'm home at last."

Baldy said. "Amen"

OTHER BOOKS WRITTEN BY
THEODORE POTTER

TRUE TALES OF ALASKA AND
THEODORE POTTER'S MEMIORS

GOLD GUNS AND TRUE LOVE

WILDSTREAK

www.ingramcontent.com/pod-product-compliance
Lightning Source LLC
Chambersburg PA
CBHW060103260626
47160CB00005B/1786